KING CHARLIE'S RIDERS

G·K Hall &Cº

Also published in Large Print
from G.K. Hall by Max Brand:

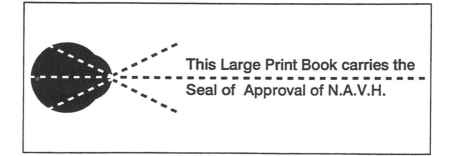

This Large Print Book carries the
Seal of Approval of N.A.V.H.

KING CHARLIE'S RIDERS

Max Brand

G.K. Hall & Co.
Thorndike, Maine

Published in Large Print by arrangement with
Golden West Literary Agency.

G.K. Hall Large Print Book Series.

Set in 16 pt. News Plantin by Barbara Ingerson.

Printed on acid free paper in the United States of America.

Library of Congress Cataloging in Publication Data

Brand, Max, 1892-1944.
    King Charlie's riders : a western story / by Max Brand.
      p. cm.
    ISBN 0-8161-5712-X (alk. paper : lg. print)
    1. Large type book. I. Title.
    [PS3511.A87K54   1993]
    813'.52—dc20   93-19645

CONTENTS

KING CHARLIE'S RIDERS

CHAPTER I

A MAN OF PREFERENCES

BEHOLD him on the top of the hill! His head is high, his eye is bright, his posture is that of a king looking down upon his own country. He is four and fifty years of age, and his birthday fell last Sunday, though he himself does not know it, for a dozen years ago he purposely lost track of time. He is four and fifty years of age, but he seems at least ten or fifteen years younger, for his step is long and elastic, his gesture quick and nervous, his voice vibrant; there is not a deep line in his brown face or a single gray hair on his head!

Who is this who has come through the desert and out of it without a pack on his back or a canteen at his side? Behind him lies that desert, a riot of color — a freak of a desert it is, having cast off those gray garments in which the mountain desert usually appears; for the sands are orange, and the rocks are black. The sky is its own heavenly blue, with dazzling white clouds blowing gayly across it. Far away, smoke trees fill a depression in the hills and flow out, winding slowly across the sands, until they seem to be a ghost river.

7

Whatever lure may be in the mountain desert, this tall fellow does not feel it.

He has turned his back on it. He is not even staring down at the little town at his feet, but far away he sees a sign of his kingdom, and his lips part in a slow smile as though he were drinking a draft of pure joy. That sign of his empire is the swiftly drifting smoke of a railroad train driving toward the horizon, and the empire of the man on the hill is the empire of the steel tracks.

Yes, he is a tramp. It is the absence of all care that has permitted his unweighted shoulders to remain so straight; and it is the absence of remorse that keeps his hair so luxuriantly thick and dark, and leaves his face unseamed.

Peering at him more closely, one may see that the skin is a little thick and rumpled over the knuckles of his hands, and that the skin of his face seems tough and dense, with a rough texture, while the high color seems stained permanently into the cheeks and cannot fade, no matter what grief or terror he may feel. Life in the open has kept him young, and when he was perforce constrained by the heavy hand of the law to live and sleep in one place for years together, his thoughts were still roving under the stars and in the wind.

He is a tramp, but never dream that this is any cold-hand-out hobo, for he is a hot-diet man. Mistake him not, at the same time, for a gay cat, one of those wretches who work from time to time when their courage as beggars fails them. Neither is he sponger upon his own kind, the lowest of the low. No, for this is the highest order.

He is no bundle stiff. He scorns to carry his blankets as he roves, but, trusting to divine chance with a courage worthy of a greater cause, he throws himself ahead on the long road and never loses heart, whatever its windings. When he begs, it is from house to house, and he does not take the first thing offered him in the matter of food. No, no; far, far from that. He is a fellow of preferences which will not down. He has been known to beg at twenty houses, because on that particular morning he felt like having sausage for breakfast and would not be content with less.

How could twenty doors be opened to him? No, rather ask: How could they remain closed when he presented himself? See how neatly he is dressed, and with what pains he now produces an old rag and wipes the desert dust from his shoes, then finds a small pocket whisk broom and gives similar attention to his hat.

Shoes and hat, those prime objects of a tramp's attention, satisfactorily attended to, he continues his work with the brush until coat, vest, and trousers have been thoroughly searched and every atom of the dust is driven off into the wind. Then he removes from around his neck the handkerchief which was there to prevent the sweat from soaking the dust into the collar of his coat.

Last he brings out a little round mirror, and in this views his face attentively from many angles, at first shaking his head dolorously, but presently plucking up more cheer and going briskly about

9

giving his features a rubbing which will almost answer the purpose of soap and water and towel.

With all this done, he looks down again on the little town, a small cattle town where the only two roofs of any importance are the red roof of the school and the blue roof of the hotel-merchandise store. His destination is the railroad yonder, which will end the curse of this long walk across country. But his next station on the journey is to be the little town immediately below him. He cocks out his elbows, inhales a deep breath, and swings off jauntily down the hills.

Such is King Charlie!

No, the picture is not yet complete, for part way down the slope he pauses to light a cigarette. From an inside coat pocket he produces a leather case, and from the case he selects a "tailor-made" smoke. He places the cigarette between his lips, and the case is restored to his pocket. He draws out, now, a match box preserved from crushing — oh, luxury — by an iron frame. He opens the box, he selects a match and lights it; but when the flaming little stick is almost at the end of the cigarette a sudden tremor seizes him. There is only that one word for it. He is *seized* as though a hand had taken him by the shoulder and were violently shaking him. From head to foot he quivers. The bright color in his cheek pales, though it does not quite go out. He makes a desperate effort, his nostrils dilating as though a great terror had fallen upon him. But still he cannot put that flame to the tobacco, and presently the match is shaken from his finger tips. He removes the cigarette next, but it also falls through his fingers to the ground.

It is the prison tremor which some men get after two or three years in the penitentiary, and which it requires fourteen or fifteen years, split up into many terms, to give to a more hardened character. It is the shaking which comes from the haunting dread that in another moment the hand of the "cop" will be clapped upon his shoulder. It is the dread of society; it is the horror of the law that is the invisible hand shaking King Charlie even here in the wilderness.

Other men get it in other places. It stops the sneak thief, perhaps, with his finger tips working at the watch. It wakens the murderer with a leap in his sleep, the sweat streaming down his forehead. It has interfered in the midst of the commission of the greatest crimes, and made the master criminal helpless. That, of course, is a rarity; and rare indeed was it to see a man with such nerves as the nerves of King Charlie broken and made to shudder by a thing which did not appear as even a wraith.

He mastered the shaking, however, after a moment of fierce effort. Perhaps it was the excitement of seeing the railroad in the distance, and the prospect just before him of the termination of his long tramp, which made him lose his nerve. He wondered grimly if the tremor would ever come to him when he was riding the rods. If so, it would be the end of King Charlie. Yet he considered that prospect without again turning pale. Real cowardice did not exist in the body of King Charlie. Out came cigarette case and matches once more, and he lighted his smoke, inhaled a deep breath of it, and snapped the smoking match into empty air with a challenge to the world to beat him yet.

Then he went on, jaunty as ever.

CHAPTER II

ON MISCHIEF BENT

He slackened his gait as he entered the town, and his face assumed a more thoughtful expression. Not that he had the slightest doubt as to his ability to secure food for the evening meal, but he had to readjust himself a little whenever he entered one of these small Western towns. There was always food in plenty to be had in one of them, but there was also an immense amount of trouble lurking for him just around the corner unless he proceeded with the most extreme care.

As he walked along the street, deep in his meditations, a voice from the side accosted him.

"H'wareye, stranger?"

"Hullo," said King Charlie, and looked up into the face of a dusty man who was reining a dusty horse toward him. Perhaps this was the man who was to take him home to food and a place to rest. He eyed the other curiously.

"What you doing this far West?" asked the man on horseback.

King Charlie was startled. This was certainly not a hospitable manner of beginning a conversation.

"I dunno why I shouldn't be this far West," he declared.

"Well," said the other without heat, "I do know a pile of reasons."

"You do? Why?"

"That ain't the point. Them reasons suit me. Besides, I seen you knocking at doors in New Wilmington a month ago."

King Charlie continued to smile as calmly as ever. "You must have me mixed up with some other gent," he said. "I dunno how —"

The other exploded with sudden wrath.

"Mind how you talk!" A hand was snapped out, and a grim forefinger pointed like a gun at the head of The King. "Mind how you talk! I've got this to back me up!" He flicked open his coat, and the expert eye of Charlie caught a glimpse of a badge of some sort. "A hobo less would be a gift to the world," declared the man on horseback. "Hanged if I ain't tempted every time I look at one. But I'll tell you what: Unless you want to land in the jail, and trot out from the jail to a woodpile for thirty days, you get out of town before night. I don't mind you so much during the day, but when I catch a bo at night I'm death on 'em!"

He waited for no answer, but twitched his horse to one side and loped down the street. A cupful of dust was scooped up by a hind hoof and flung into the air, where it dissolved into a cloud that blew straight into the face of King Charlie. He busied himself removing all traces of that dust before he permitted himself to think, far less speak.

14

Then he said to himself: "For that I'll get even with your town! You're a watchdog, are you? Bah! I'll steal half the town right under your nose!" And The King snapped his fingers carelessly in the air.

After trying one or two doors, however, he became more concerned. The doors were locked, and there seemed hardly a soul in town. Of course he could get into any of those houses that he wished to enter, but he had not the slightest desire to commit burglary by forcing a lock when he had no idea of what the lock might be guarding.

Then he learned the cause of the exodus. There was a bucking contest on the outskirts of the village; and, indeed, from the top of the hill he remembered now that he had noted a drift of men and horses out of the town.

"They're picking the best rider out of Carterville," said the old woman who was his informant. "And they're going to send him down to the State bucking contest, with all expenses paid. It's about time we folks waked up and done something like that. There's Saunderstown and Four Oaks on each side of us have won the prize two years running. And we got better men right here than ever was growed in Saunderstown and Four Oaks put together."

"You certainly have, ma'am," observed King Charlie. "Everybody inside of five hundred miles has heard some sort of mention of Carterville."

He found that the grounds for the bucking affair had been laid out in a small pasture on the verge of the village. Around the fence two or three hundred men, women, and children were gathered, and above their heads drifted a mist of fine dust, now and then reenforced with a great outburst, white as a cloud; and from time to time the hoofs of horses thudded in broken rhythm on the ground, and the snorting of horses was heard as they landed with all their force in crooked positions.

But these noises and the shouting of the spectators had ceased as The King came up with the onlookers and squeezed a way to the fence between an old and a young woman. He saw that in one corner of the lot were corralled a dozen ugly-looking horses, wild as the wind, every one of them.

They were sweating with fear, and some of them bore the marks of the saddles which had been cinched on them. But for that matter, the riders bore even more distinct marks. Here was one with a rag bound around a face as swollen as though he were afflicted with the mumps; and yonder was another who limped feebly, supporting himself with one hand resting on the fence.

"Them Dirks hosses is sure man-killers!" the old man at The King's right remarked with a chuckle. "My, my! This reminds me of the days when —"

"But think of that little Billy English having got clean into the finals!" cried the girl, interrupting.

The King made out that he had worked his way in between two members of a single family. He eyed them nonchalantly. The old man's lower right vest pocket was bulging with a big watch, but the practiced eye of The King estimated from the rim, which was visible, that it was plated gold only. At the front of the girl's dress was a diamond pin, but the jewel was not worth twenty dollars. He would not risk such petty thefts in so small a crowd or so far from the railroad.

"He ain't so little," said the old man.

"Why, dad, he's only fourteen!"

"Well, when I was a boy fourteen, I was old enough to do a man's work. I recollect well milking twelve cows night and morning, besides plowing all day long — when I was under fourteen. Yes, sir! Little Billy English ain't so little, after all. He's as tall as you be, Bess, or my name ain't Lester!"

"Nonsense, dad!"

The testy old gentleman shook his head and stamped. "Tush!" he said. "The idees of you women —"

"Hush!"

"Well?"

"See them shake hands! They're going to ride it off. They're going to ride off the tie! See Billy and Joe Fairview shake hands over yonder? They're going to fight it out to a finish!"

"No — no!" muttered the ancient, peering first through his glasses and then over them. "You ain't telling me that, are you?"

The King followed the direction of all the staring eyes around him and at once found the center of interest.

17

A tall, hard-featured cow-puncher was in the act of shaking hands with a tow-headed youngster who swung his sombrero in his other hand, and whose whole manner was that of one embarked on a tremendous lark. His blue eyes shone, and their blueness could be distinguished even at that distance. This, beyond a doubt, was little Billy English.

But as the old man had said, he was not so very small. He was already, in his fourteenth year, a matter of five or six inches over five feet. Moreover, it was not a purely gawky height. His shoulders were both wide and well rounded out, and every move of his body and gesture of his hand indicated lithe muscles at play in his young body. Indeed, to the keen eye of The King, practiced in estimating the abilities of pugilists, Billy English seemed rather a little man than a big boy.

"And look, dad!" cried Bess. "They're bringing out the big brown hoss! It's going to be a quick decision, no matter who wins!"

"A quick decision or a broken neck, if it's the brown hoss," muttered her father. "The judges must be tired of watching the riding if they're ordering out that hoss so quick!"

CHAPTER III

TO THE LAST INCH

THE KING now observed that three men were furiously engaged in the labor of capturing a long-legged brown horse who battled with insensate fury, knocking the humans about as though they were tenpins — except that these tenpins clung by means of ropes whose hold could not be slipped. At length the brown was down, blindfolded, and eventually saddled and brought out, dancing and fretting himself into a foam while the crowd of on-lookers gasped.

A bulky man robed in a light linen duster now advanced toward the center of the arena.

"Ladies and gents," he said, when his raised hand had brought silence to the circle around the fence, "you've all seen how Joe Fairview and Billy English have rode to a tie. Leastwise, that's the way me and the other two judges make it out. We all voted for a tie, and now that tie has got to be rode off. We're picking a bad one to try out the two gents that are still competing for the honor of representing Carterville.

"Jim Dandy is the hoss they got to ride, and the first thing is to see if each of them can stay on Jim Dandy's back for one minute without no

19

spurs locked nor leather pulling, but riding straight up and taking what's coming to 'em according to the rules. The gent that does the first riding is apt to get the worst of Jim Dandy's work, so we're going to pick him by tossing a coin. All right, ladies and gents. You won't need to start hollering to make Jim Dandy buck. He'll do his best all by his own self! The gent ain't yet showed up that's been able to rake him fore and aft while riding, and they's been a hundred of the best that's tried to stick to Jim Dandy."

He waved in conclusion and went back to his post, where the brown was now prepared for his test. Next, little Billy English and tall Joe Fairview stepped forth to see the coin flipped up from the broad thumb nail of the judge. A rush of whispers came from the onlookers.

"I can't help praying that Joe has to ride the hoss first," said Bess at The King's elbow.

"Don't make no difference," declared her testy father. "The kid ain't got a chance."

There was in The King something which responded with a thrill at the thought of a lost cause and those who maintained it. Staring across the space of blazing sunlight at the tow-headed youngster, he felt that unfamiliar leap of his heart in sympathy. Not a dozen times before in the long course of his life had The King been so stirred to hope that luck would fall to the share of any one other than himself.

Who would have to ride the formidable horse first?

The judge delayed as long as possible, to draw out the suspense before he snapped up the coin. The two contestants involuntarily leaned back to see the coin rise to the top of its arc and hang there for a glittering, winking instant before it fell in a streak of light to the dust. Then they leaned to examine it and read their destiny.

But it was deep in the dust. The judge got laboriously to his knees, blew the dust away in a great cloud, and then removed all doubt as to who was the winner by jumping up and clapping his hand on the shoulder of Joe Fairview.

Little Billy English waved his hand to his competitor in sign that he accepted the judgment of chance without malice against the successful man. Then he clapped his loose-brimmed sombrero on his head and hitched up his belt before and behind, leaning forward the while and staring at the brown horse in so aggressive an attitude that The King stepped a long stride forward and hung his arms over the top rail.

"There's a gamester!" he breathed in devout admiration. "Oh, he's a hundred and thirty pounds of iron and fire, that Billy boy!" He turned abruptly to the ancient Lester. "Who is the boy?"

"I don't know." It was the girl who answered, thinking the question addressed to her. "Well, I know as much as any one knows. He just happened into town when he was about five years old, and said that he'd walked in from the railroad. Of course every one tried to find out who his father was, but we couldn't learn. And after a time, Mr. Shaw took him in."

"Well," said The King, "he done a good job in raising that kid. I suppose he's out here giving Billy a cheer? Where is the old boy?"

"He ain't here," said the girl, laughing without mirth. "And I guess he wouldn't give his own son, if he had one, a cheer. He ain't that kind. Yes, it may have looked good of him to take in Billy when Billy was five years old, but every one says that Mr. Shaw was simply foresighted. In three years Billy was doing as many chores as a grown man could have done, almost! Mr. Shaw has hardly given him a chance to go to school in the winters! And for the last three or four years Billy has rode the range just like any grown man. Every one says it's a shame!"

"Then why doesn't somebody do something?"

"I dunno," said Bess, troubled at the thought. "I guess they don't want to get into trouble with Mr. Shaw. He's such a fierce man, you know."

"Huh!" grunted The King. "Then why don't Billy run away?"

"Why, I guess he's never thought of doing that."

"Then —" But The King left this final thought unexpressed, and turned rather abruptly to watch Billy English climb into the saddle.

In another instant the long-legged brown was off, unrestrained by bit and bridle, leaning into his longest stride with his long, ugly neck thrust out, snake-like, and his ears flattened. Never in his life had King Charlie seen so ugly a head.

Inside of half a dozen jumps, having gained enough impetus to suit himself, the outlaw flung himself high into the air and began such a set of antics that old Lester cried out: "Boys, boys, boys! Never in my days have I seen such educated pitching — eh, Bess?"

"Look! Look!" cried Bess. "He's using the spurs!"

"By George!" shouted her father, taking off his hat. "By George, lass, you're right! He's raking him fore and aft, too!"

The rules of good, honest bucking are that each rider shall not only endeavor to stick in the saddle, but he shall also do his utmost to induce the horse he sits upon to display its worst wares. Merely to ride straight up is often a small thing, but a horse which will hardly buck at all under straight riding may hurl itself into a maelstrom of bucking at the first scratch of the spurs. And little Billy English was urging Jim Dandy to do his utmost.

Swinging his legs, he ran his spurs the entire length of the body of the brown, rolling the rowel along the hide and driving Jim Dandy into a perfect frenzy. More than this, to pile Ossa on Pelion, he swung his ragged hat, and with it slapped Jim Dandy alternately between the ears and on the flanks.

It seemed to The King, as the outlaw horse reached the height of his efforts, that the air was converted into a semisolid — that it was at least like water, in which Jim Dandy turned and twisted and writhed like a fish, and ever and anon dropped down and struck the earth a tremendous blow that knocked the head of the rider forward or back or to the side. Every one of these terrific shocks must have been like the thud of a great fist against the brain of the boy.

"What's the time — what's the time on him!" cried The King, thrown into a wild excitement. "They ought to stop it. It's more than a minute. It's two minutes he's been riding!"

"Thirty seconds!" replied old Lester, glancing down at his watch.

Indeed, every man around the fence was alternately yelling and then glancing at his watch. Beyond a doubt every one wished to see the boy conquer.

"Look!" cried The King, all his poise gone in a flash. "Look at him! He's sick!"

Those merciless shocks had forced a thin trickle of crimson from the nostrils of Billy English. Now his head rocked wildly. His face was convulsed with desperate effort, and yet not for an instant did he relax his beating of the hat and his raking with the spurs to keep Jim Dandy at the height of his work. Suddenly — it was a spin of the brown, a leap into the air, and a side spring that did it — the young horseman was hurled from the saddle. No easy, slipping fall it was; he darted as a stone from a sling, and amid a yell of dismay he turned over and over on the ground.

"He's killed!" cried King Charlie.

Now Billy English leaped up, shook back his hair, clapped onto his head the sombrero upon

24

which he had never relaxed his grip, and started racing toward the brown, shrilly calling: "I'll get you this time, you long-legged sinner!"

The burst of laughter from the audience — laughter which came from relief as well as amusement — stopped him and recalled him to the fact that he had fought his fight and finished his chance. Instantly he stopped, brushed the stains from his cheek with a careless flourish of his bandanna, and cried to Joe Fairview: "Good luck, Joe!"

"Game — game to the last inch," muttered The King. "And made of India rubber, too. You could drop that kid off a cliff, and he'd land on his feet and laugh at you! He looks lucky!"

CHAPTER IV

STRAIGHT TALK

WHAT time?" breathed The King next, wiping the perspiration from his brow.

"Fifty," said old Lester. "He only lacked ten seconds. Only ten. I misdoubt that Joe can stick to Jim Dandy that long — unless the kid has taken some of the buck out of Jim."

That, however, was apparently what had happened. Joe Fairview rode well and honorably. He urged the brown horse with beating hat and raking spurs just as the boy had done, though with much less fury of gusto; but it seemed that Jim Dandy, and very rightly, considered that a day's work had been done. He bucked only twice as hard as an ordinary horse could buck, and the result was that the dauntless Joe lasted through the sixty seconds and then slipped out of the saddle victorious.

Straight across the field walked tow-headed Billy English, thrust out his hand, and shook that of the victor with a broad grin. Then he sauntered toward the fence, swung himself over it with much agility, and, still smiling and laughing at those who crowded around him offering condolences and praise, he declared that he must hurry home to finish some chores. He disappeared straightaway down the street while the others turned their attention to the man of the hour, Joe Fairview, who was now to carry their hopes and their ambitions to the State Fair.

That is, all turned toward him saving one man among the spectators, and that was The King. He detached himself from his place at the fence, glided through the crowd with the ease of an eel through muddy water, and started down the street in pursuit at his long, swinging stride which devoured distance with an amazing speed. Fast runners may be made, but fast walkers must be born and then made afterward.

He touched the shoulder of Billy English in a few moments, and the latter turned toward him a white, smiling face — with the expression just a little set.

"You're pretty sick, ain't you, son?" asked The King.

There was a sudden change in the expression of the boy. The smile vanished and left him wan and with his forehead covered with a clammy sweat.

"I'm all right," he gasped out.

"Come in here," insisted The King, and showed the way between two houses and behind a shed, leading Billy English with a grasp which the latter had no apparent strength to resist. "Now lie down," he ordered when they reached their destination — a small stretch of dead grasses.

Billy English slumped down and lay flat on his back, his eyes closed, his nostrils dilated, his lips parted and gasping for air. The tramp watched him with quiet concern. Then he opened the boy's shirt at the throat, pulled the shirt out, and fanned rapidly with his hat so that a current of air passed over Billy's chest.

After a moment the boy was able to gasp out through his teeth: "Thanks! I'm all right now!"

"The devil you are!" said The King quietly. "You stay right where you are till I tell you to move."

It was ten minutes before Billy English sat up and flushed with shame as he looked at the tramp.

"I dunno how it was," he confessed. "I got sort of sick."

"At the stomach, eh?" asked King Charlie.

"That's it, Mr. —"

"Smith — Charles Smith."

"I guess it was the sun that got to working on me, Mr. Smith," said the boy.

The title affected Charlie oddly. It was long since he had been a mister, far longer than he had been a king.

"The sun, eh?" he murmured. "I don't suppose the bucking had anything to do with it?"

"Oh, no. I just lost a stirrup, that's all."

"You'd like to try it over again, maybe, now that you are rested up — and Jim Dandy is rested up, too."

The boy flushed, and his eyes gleamed. "Will they give me another whirl?" he breathed.

"You can't go to ride in the State fair, anyway."

"I know that, but me and Jim Dandy ain't had

it out yet, you can bet on that!"

King Charlie answered curtly: "You've had your chance, and you weren't good enough to take it."

"I ain't whining," said Billy English, rising to his feet and shaking himself together. "Next time — well, so long."

"Wait a minute. Where're you going?"

"Why d'you ask?"

"I got particular reasons for wanting to know."

"Why, I'm going home, that's all."

"And what you going to do when you get there?"

"What business is that of yours?"

"Look here, son, how much older am I than you?"

The boy flushed and cleared his throat. "Well," he said, recognizing that age gave the other the right to talk to him and ask as many questions as he chose, "when I get home I'll get to work. They's a string of cows to be milked before night, and every one of 'em is my work."

"D'you always work when you're at home?"

"Why, no. I live the same as everybody else. That's my home, you see. I sleep and eat there, and everything."

"You sleep and eat and work there seven days a week?"

"Why, not on Sundays —"

"You milk the string of cows on Sunday, don't you?"

"Ye-es."

He seemed vastly reluctant to admit that he had duties even on the day of rest.

"And besides, if they's anything turns up that has to be done on Sunday you're the one that does it, ain't you? Extra wood — or a fence to be mended, or anything the like of that?"

"Sure. That's only nacheral, me being the youngest man around."

"So that on Sundays you're about as busy as any other day?"

"That can't be helped."

"Well, I suppose you get good pay, working seven days a week that way," the older man hinted.

"Pay? Why, nobody gets paid for working in their own home."

"Don't they? What makes a home a home?"

"Why, it's where your father and mother lives and —"

"*Your* father and mother?" King Charlie asked.

"Well, not exactly. Mr. Shaw took me in, though, which makes him have a pile more claim on me than most fathers have on their own sons!"

"I guess Shaw has told you that pretty often."

The boy flushed. "Well?" he asked, strictly on the defensive.

"To make it short — that ain't your home any more than it is mine. If Shaw wants to treat you like a son, why don't he adopt you and give you his own name and make you heir to his land and house? Why don't he do that?"

The boy paused. He was unable to answer. He lapsed into a brown study, and The King gave him time to think, for that blackening forehead meant a storm ahead for Mr. Shaw.

At length there had passed a sufficient space of silence, in the judgment of The King. He rose, walked to a pile of tin cans, selected one, and tossed it, without warning, high in the air and to a considerable distance.

"Hit that!" he cried while the can was at the height of its rise.

Automatically the boy obeyed. He was in an awkward position, with his arms folded and his hands as far as possible from the butt of his gun. But the weapon came out like a flash, and just before the tin can struck the ground the weapon exploded, and the can darted off in a long, straight, sparkling line under the ringing impact.

Billy put up the gun with an exclamation.

"That was a fool thing to do," he said.

But The King walked over, picked up the can, and examined the hole, exactly in the center.

"It was a mighty hard thing to do," he commented quietly.

CHAPTER V

KING CHARLIE WINS

As he turned toward the boy again, his mind was made up. Billy English must go with him. From the first moment when his eyes had fallen on the boy something had leaped up in him in recognition. It was not the mere exhibition of modesty and courage and skill combined which he had witnessed in the horse riding and again in this small but significant bit of gun play that influenced him he told himself. It was more, far more.

Every rascal likes to feel that there are mysterious impulses behind his rascality. Yet, having made up his mind, the tramp hesitated before he ventured on the one real hold — in appearance — which he might use to bring Billy along with him.

"I got to be going now," Billy was saying. "I sure can't stay any longer, Mr. Smith. Mr. Shaw'll be plumb mad if —"

"Well? Let him hire somebody, why don't you? Or let him hire you. Ain't I convinced you that you deserve wages, anyway?"

Billy pondered and then raised his thoughtful face.

"I guess I do," he said. "I hadn't thought —

but I guess I do deserve 'em, and I guess I'll get 'em!"

"You think so, eh? What sort of wages will you ask for?"

"Man wages!"

"Not half wages?"

"Half wages?" He drew himself up proudly. "I ain't very big," he admitted, "but I ain't so small, either. I can rope a cow as fast as most, ride as well as a few, handle a gun in a pinch, run a plow, milk a cow if they's a herd of milkers — not that I'm extra good at any of them things; but I do as well as most, I think."

"So you think you'd ought to get full-sized wages?"

"That kind or none at all."

"H'm," murmured The King. "Well, you go tell Shaw right now what you want. I'll wait here till you come back."

The boy frowned.

"But what makes you think that I'll come back?"

"When you get through telling Shaw what you want, and he gets through telling you what he thinks of what you want, you'll be ready to come back here."

"Why should I come here?"

"Because I'll be waiting here with a pretty good idea of what you'd ought to do next."

The boy hesitated. Several times he seemed on the verge of speaking. Then without a word he turned and hurried toward the street.

As for The King, he settled himself philosophically in the sun — for it was now near evening, and in the approaching night chill the yellow sunlight possessed a grateful warmth — and waited for the development of events.

He consulted his watch. Twenty minutes had passed, then half an hour, then forty minutes. He began to grow alarmed. Had the youngster lost his nerve at the last moment? He had not seemed that kind. But, then, one could never tell. Shaw might be a shrewd old fellow with a great hold over the imagination of the boy. And boys are all imagination.

What was happening?

A full hour ran out, and the sun was a bulging disk of red balanced on top of a western hill when a shrill whistling came up the street, turned a corner, and behold! There stood Billy English with gun belt, canteen, and a small roll of blankets thrown over his shoulder. Best of all, he was laughing.

What a trump the youngster was, thought the tramp.

"Well?" asked King Charlie.

"He sure had a lot to say," the boy remarked, and chuckled. "He told me that it plumb busted his heart to hear of such ingratitude as mine — me having been reared tender and careful by him. He got so sorry for himself that the tears came up in his eyes. I was afraid that he was going to bust out crying. Well, I sort of weakened, but I kept saying that I thought I'd ought to get paid for my work. Then he tried a new line with me,

34

just like a hoss that switches from fence-rowing to sun-fishing. He got dignified.

" 'How much money a month d'you think you're worth?' he asks me.

" 'Forty dollars with board and keep,' says I. "He lets out a yell at that.

" 'You young limb of Satan!' he hollers. 'Are you trying to hold me up and rob me?'

" 'Well,' says I, getting sort of mad, but leading him on, 'how much d'you think I am worth?'

" 'I hadn't ought to give you nothing,' says Shaw. 'But I suppose if you want to drag money out of a poor man's pocket I could afford to pay you five dollars a month.'

"Well, I laughed in his face at that, and he began to storm. I turned around and went up to my room. Pretty soon he come and followed me. I heard him and locked the door. He stood outside and started begging. It made me sick to hear him. I sure have been a fool, living with that old hound all these years and never guessing what sort of gent he was when he bullied me and kept driving me to work.

"He started by offering me seven dollars and a half a month. He said he couldn't afford that much, and that I wasn't worth that much, but that he was so fond of me that something come over him at the idea of me going.

"I told him I knew what had come over him, and it was a terrible shock to think of what he'd have to pay in board and keep and wages to two full-growed men that he would have to hire to

35

do the work that I'd been doing for nothing.

"At that he let out a yell and started in telling how hard he'd worked when he was a boy, but I let him yell and kept on looking around for the things that I owned, because I was plumb set on not taking with me anything that the old man had bought for me —"

"H'm," broke in King Charlie at this point. "That sounds sort of foolish to me, Billy."

"How could I keep anything when I was leaving him?" asked Billy.

The tramp waved to him to continue.

"Then he worked up to the point where he was offering me thirty dollars a month and keep and Sundays off. The old scoundrel! Then I threw the door open and walked up to him and told him a few truths about himself, and what a skunk he'd been to work the skin off of me all these years — just the way you told me how to talk. And Shaw? He just curled up, the yaller sneak!"

The boy burned with righteous indignation.

"When I was leaving, Shaw locked the door behind me and then cussed me through the window and told me that he'd always hated the sight of me, but that he'd got a couple of thousand dollars' worth of work out of me, and that was the only reason he'd kept me. He wished me bad luck — yep, he's a sure-enough bad one!"

Then he added, seeing a curious expression in the face of the tramp: "And now what?"

"They's a gent here that seems to want to talk to me," said The King uneasily.

The boy turned. "Why that's the sheriff. Hello!" he called to the dusty rider.

The latter waved a cheerful greeting, or at least a greeting as near cheer as he ever could come. The wide disk of the sun was half down.

"You got half a minute," said the sheriff to King Charlie, "to start out of town."

The King bowed with vast dignity. He hated the sheriff with all his heart for having come at all, but above all for having arrived at this moment, of all moments the most inopportune.

"You got power on your side, sheriff," he said sadly. "I ain't got the strength to stand against you."

The sheriff frowned, then glanced quickly at Billy English. This speech was made for effect — that was plain. And therefore it must be made for its effect on Billy English.

"Why ain't you at home doing your chores?" he asked a little too sharply, as even the most kindly men will occasionally speak to a child.

But Billy English considered himself well past childhood, and though there was no conceit in his honest young head, he felt that his work of the afternoon entitled him to a great deal of extra consideration.

"I'm through doing chores for old Shaw," he said carelessly. "He's had enough charity work done for him."

"H'm," said the sheriff.

"Besides," went on the boy, "I'm kind of curious, sheriff, to find out what you got agin' my friend, Mr. Smith."

"Is that his name?" asked the sheriff, turning a grim eye on King Charlie.

The latter saw that he would have to fight for his prize before he carried it off.

"It is," said the boy, "and grinning won't change that name a mite —"

For the sheriff was faintly smiling.

"It won't?" echoed the sheriff in a tone which might be taken to imply many things.

"Nor it won't stop him from being my friend," said Billy stoutly, driven by the sheriff's recalcitrant attitude further than he had intended to go.

"The name I know him by," said the sheriff, at length, "is King Charlie."

"What's that nickname got to do with him?"

"You've never heard of him?"

"Never!"

"You're a bright kid, Billy, but they's a pile of things that you ain't never heard of yet. A million folks know King Charlie, the tramp!"

Billy turned on the stranger like a flash. In all his hard-working young life he had come to know of nothing more detestable to him than the bare hint of a tramp, a professional idler, living on the labors of honest folk like himself.

"Is that true?" he asked bitterly. "Are you — what the sheriff says?"

King Charlie was fairly cornered. He could not fight his way out by dint of argument, but he must trust to evasion to extricate him from the contempt of Billy English. He took off his hat and bowed

38

with ironic politeness to the sheriff.

"Him being the sheriff," he said, "he must be right."

"Don't say that," said Billy, "but tell me the truth!"

"No use," said King Charlie with affectation of vast sadness. "You'd take his word before you'd take mine."

"I wouldn't!" cried Billy. "Your word means as much to me as the word of any man — until you've proved yourself something I can't trust."

It was such a copy-book sentiment that King Charlie dared not meet the fierce eye of the sheriff. In spite of himself he shrank in shame. It was indeed cruel to persuade this youngster to go off with him. And yet the prize was great. He was, he had to admit, no longer as young as he had once been, and supposing that he could convert the boy to his way of living — as, with his superior mental training and powers of persuasion, plus age, he should easily be able to do — he would be providing a "staff and a comforter" for himself in days to come. Besides, something within him yearned toward the brave youngster. Rascal that he was, he could not but love the fine honesty of the boy.

"Let the sheriff call me what he can," said The King. "I know myself. I ain't ashamed of what I am. Poor, yes. Homeless, yes. A wanderer, yes. But not without a good, honest pride, I thank Heaven. Not without that, I pray!"

Of course, it meant nothing in words; the tone

was everything, and the tone threw a glitter into the eyes of Billy English.

"You hear that?" he demanded of the sheriff.

"I hear him making a fool of you, Billy. Are you going to believe such crazy talk as that?"

"I'll be a judge of that," said Billy, dark with dignity. "Maybe I ain't a sheriff, but it don't follow that I'm a fool, I hope."

The King instantly seized the opening. "He's a terrible wise man, your sheriff. He sees right through you and me, Billy. He sees that we ain't no good, but he's sure got his nerve with him to stand up and talk about it the way he does! If I was younger —"

"You old villain!" cried the sheriff. "You sneaking rascal, Charlie! What are you planning to do with the kid here?"

Charlie turned to the boy with a gesture. "Will you listen to that?" he asked. "As if I could do anything with you that I felt like doing! Is that sense?"

"Charlie!" cried the sheriff. "The sun is down. Get out of town, and get out quick!"

Again Charlie removed his hat and bowed as to tyrannous authority. He turned to Billy and extended his hand.

"So long, son," he said. "I only wish that I'd had a chance to know you better."

"You'll have that chance," said Billy, brushing the hand to one side and glaring at the sheriff. "You'll have that chance if you don't mind me going along with you."

The heart of the tramp leaped into his throat. Was he not carrying out his threat of taking from the town something from under the very nose of the sheriff?

"Come — and welcome, son," he said in a voice shaken by triumph and a truly kindly emotion.

"Billy, you little fool!" roared the sheriff. "What you aiming to do? Go with that old buzzard?"

But Billy snapped his fingers. "Seems to me," he said hotly, "that you're using an awful pile of strong words, sheriff, and the next time you call me a fool I'll be thanking you if you have your hand near your gun."

"Why, you young idiot," cried the sheriff, "you need a licking, that's what you need!"

"Start giving it," said Billy, swinging a little from side to side in a very ecstasy of passion. "Start in! And I'll cuss you to start you off!"

He stood there with his knees flexed a little, a lithe, taut figure that, motionless, suggested more speed than another in full action. The sheriff missed not a line of that body and attitude. He studied Billy English with curiosity and sadness commingled, for in his own harsh way he was a kindly man.

"You're going to go, then?"

"D'you think that you can stop me?"

"No, Billy," said the sheriff. "But if you've set your mind on that, all I ask you to remember is that when we found you, a little four-year-old shaver, you was all dressed up fine, Billy. You looked like the son of high-class folks. And you

41

talked bright as a dollar and used better English than I'm using right now. I'm asking you to remember them things when you step out with The King. Keep your hands clean!"

Billy English favored him with a parting glare.

"I'll try to take care of myself without your help," he declared. "Come along, Mr. Smith."

King Charlie turned and removed his hat to the sheriff for the third time, and a smile of malice and triumph was curling his lips.

CHAPTER VI

A TEST OF NERVE

As they went along the road at a good clip, heading direct for the railroad, Billy English noted the walking powers of his new acquaintance with admiration. Himself reared to a life in the saddle, the only flaw in his otherwise neatly made young body being the slight bow of his legs from constant riding, he knew nothing of traveling in any other manner than in a saddle. But King Charlie swung along with a faultless roll from hip to heel and toe, fairly shooting himself along at such a pace that Billy English had to stretch to a half run from time to time.

They hurried up a long slope and came close to the railroad in this fashion, and by the rails King Charlie paused. Here he eyed his young friend askance. Billy English was panting so heavily that his chest was a veritable bellows, but he did not make a single murmur of complaint.

The King saw and understood. The test meant much to him. If the boy had complained of the rate of their walk or spoken enviously of the long legs of his companion or made an excuse about sore feet, the good opinion of The King would have been half destroyed on the instant. But, instead, that resolute silence and the glance which unflinchingly went up the steeper slope beyond the rails made the heart of the tramp leap again with pleasure.

Here was metal — here was certainly finest steel. Oh, to have the molding of this youngster into a man, a destroyer of society just as he, King Charlie, had been!

"Here's where we get a lift if you're coming along with me," said The King.

"Where?" asked the boy. "There's no road near here that I see."

"Ain't there a railroad here?"

"But no station. Besides, I haven't a penny for a ticket."

The King rubbed his long, bony hands together. How strange to find a half-grown boy who did not know that the railroad was the great free highway on which the only tickets needed were courage and a certain measure of address!

He raised a hand: "Listen!"

"I can't hear nothing," said Billy English.

"Listen again! Hear that humming and whining, sort of beyond the edge of the sky?"

"Yes, yes!"

"That's a train coming — a freight, too, I guess. If it is, you and me take it, son!"

He estimated the grade. Yes, the train would, if it were a loaded freight, be climbing this grade so slowly that they could take it, even though the leap might be a hard one to make.

So, having done enough to kindle the interest

of the boy, he said not another word; and although Billy was writhing with curiosity and impatience he immediately adopted the laconic attitude of his new-found friend and maintained the same silence.

As they sat in the screen of bushes near the track, they saw the front of the tall engine rock around the curve below them, with a thin screen of steam and smoke dragging behind the chimney. That screen, as the fireman fed up to give the engine full power on the grade, turned into a coughing black that puffed up a dozen feet above the smokestack and then was caught by the wind of the engine's speed and snatched away in a line parallel with the earth.

"It sure ain't going to stop," said the boy, instinctively crouching a little and making himself smaller at the sight of that monster engine.

The King listened with keen ear. That heavy rumble meant a loaded string of twenty-five or thirty cars, and, if so, he would make an effort to board the train. Billy English must follow; for he could estimate, from the manner in which the engine grew out at them, that the train was not coming too swiftly for an expert to mount it.

It mattered not that Billy was not an expert, he told himself grimly, it mattered not that he was only a boy; for if he were to be capable of the great things which The King was already sketching dimly and in loose strokes for the future, he must be capable of doing whatever within reason was asked of him.

"There we are," said The King complacently.

45

"There she comes, Billy. Does she look good enough to ride on, to you?"

"But — does she stop here?"

"Stop? Sure she doesn't. But you and me ain't going to worry about that. We'll jump for it, eh?"

Billy English looked at his companion with a wan smile, as though ready to appreciate the joke; but when he saw The King already looking with an earnest eye at the approaching train he turned entirely displeased; he was simply anxious. He did not want any thick-skinned clod, unafraid because he did not know what fear was. He wanted a keenly sensitive and alert organism. Only such could prove worth the schooling which The King intended for the boy.

"Jump for it?" echoed Billy.

"Aim at one of the ladders, them iron ladders going up the side of the car," said The King negligently. "When you jump, you bunch your feet and your hands together. You aim at one step with all four, because you can be pretty sure that your hands will hit above the one you aim at with your feet. If you do that way, you got a good chance of swinging on. If one foot misses, the other will most likely land. If one hand misses, the other will be pretty apt to catch on. And there you are. Another thing: When you jump, take a run as fast as you can go alongside the train the same way that the train is running; but when you jump, turn in toward the train and jump straight at it, just as if you were going to punch a hole clean through the box car. Understand?"

He illustrated the maneuvers with little brusque gestures, and Billy English listened with his teeth setting hard, although his face was colorless.

"Listen to 'em roar!" muttered the old tramp, half closing his eyes. "Listen to them cars come, lad. They got some empties in that string, too. You can tell 'em by the sort of hollow ring they got, a whole lot higher than the rumble of a loaded car. Now she comes! Let 'er go — let 'er shoot — oh, beauty!"

The enthusiasm of King Charlie waxed to an epic intensity as he heard the train roar more and more loudly — oh, sound so welcome after the hot silence of the desert and the endless sands!

"Watch me — then you do the trick, Billy!" cried The King, and, so saying, he rolled to his feet with surprising quickness and scurried down the line several rods, under cover of the brush. He was at length at a considerable distance, and Billy English, watching with unspeakable concern, saw The King, as the monster freight panted past, dart out of his hiding place and race like the wind beside the train, then face sharply in and leap, catlike, straight at the car, with feet and hands, as he had said, bunched closely together. When he struck on the iron rounds of the ladder up the side of an empty box car the impetus of the train swung him far to one side, so that only a faultless grip with his hands and his feet and flexible wrists as well, enabled him to hang there without his grip being broken.

But in another moment he had righted himself

and slipped up the ladder. There he remained, with his head barely above the top of the car, waving toward Billy and making cheering signals.

Yet Billy English paused, panting hard. There was no reason for him to make this leap into the teeth of danger except to please a vagrant stranger who should mean nothing to him. There was, indeed, no reason at all.

Besides, there was something dangerous in the tall stranger — something dangerously attractive. He had a manner too persuasive. It had seemed to Billy that if the tall man cared to exert himself, he, Billy English, would be forced by sheer weight of words to act as his preceptor bade him act. He could not stand up against the subtle and fluid talk of The King. Better stay far away from him!

The big engine swayed past him, grinding up that rough road, dripping hot oil and spurting steam from laboring pistons. Inside the cabin was the engineer with his black visor drawn aslant across his worn, care-stricken, young-old face. And behind him he saw, as the cab rolled past, the fireman, a gay-faced Irishman with his mouth agape over a song, not a murmur of which was audible above the mighty groaning and rushing of the train.

On came the long line of the train, the noise of grinding and clanking wheels a comparative silence the moment the engine was by. Each set of wheels had a different note; each clanked by with a diminishing racket as the distance to the engine increased.

And yonder was the figure — jaunty in spite of its age — of The King, clinging with only one hand, his weight resting on one foot while he waved his hat in gay invitation toward the boy.

Billy English groaned, averted his eyes, and through what seemed to him an age he waited for that figure to pass. But when he looked up again with a guilty start — behold, the form was still in view.

There seemed a fate in it. He could not be tried and found lacking by a man who should be far past the age of agility! Settling his strong, lithe young shoulders under his pack, jerking his belt and the dependent holster more snugly about his waist, Billy English gave a tug to his hat, and then turned out into the open and sprinted ahead faster than he had ever sprinted before.

But his speed was almost nothing. Still the line of freight cars strung out ahead of him, floating easily away, and as he raced so close beneath the train he could the better estimate its surprising speed. One car went past him with a swish and a short wink of open air and sunlight on the far side; another whisked past, and then he saw The King coming, shouting inaudible words.

Suppose he were to leap and fall short, or suppose he missed his grip? It mattered not, for he would swing in — swing in and under, and the smoothly spinning wheels would shear him in two!

Yet he turned in with a sudden short cry of desperation and a furious, determined mind. So, his face convulsed with effort, he hurled himself as high and as far into the air as he could, and to such purpose that, the next he knew, he had crashed flat into the side of the car and received on face and chest a crushing blow. His feet slipped from the round at which he had aimed them, and the velocity of the train's forward motion left him clinging by no more than one handgrip!

CHAPTER VII

A PRODIGIOUS LIE

HE trailed to one side, flung out like a flag by the speed of the train, and he felt his left hand, by which he clung, slipping, with a strain cast on the wrist that threatened to splinter the bones.

If he made another effort, in all probability he would wrench himself from his hold. But he had to fasten that grip or fall. Across the top of the freight car, racing at full speed with marvelous disregard of the uneasy, rocking footing to which he had intrusted himself, came The King; but in spite of his speed he could come too late. Billy's destruction or salvation depended on himself.

He was swinging back now toward a normal hanging position, and as he swung he reached with his right arm. Naturally it worked his numbed left hand loose, and the fingers slipped entirely from their hold. With all his might he reached and gripped with his right hand, but he failed of his hold, and it was a round lower where both left and right hand secured a lodging.

The wrench nearly tore his shoulders from his body, but the double grip supported him. All of this had happened in the space of five seconds from his leap. Now he dragged himself up on the ladder, found kneehold and then foothold, and eventually clung to it, upright, with a dizzy feeling of sickness.

Here the hand of The King was reached to him, and he dragged himself up to the top. He was paralyzed still with the reaction from his fear, and he half expected to find The King laughing at his pale face. But instead he was surprised to see that The King himself was by no means ruddy. He clutched Billy and dragged him down on the top of the car.

"That gave me the worst scare I ever had in my life," he panted out. "By thunder, Billy, I'm all in with it — all in!"

In fact, he looked it. The permanent patch of color high in either cheek was now no more than a faded purple, and his breath still came in gasps as though his had been the exertion and not Billy's. A brakeman presently found them. He balanced back on his heels as the train shot around a sharp turn, the wind making his hickory shirt cling to his body as though soaked in water.

"That was a close one," he said, grinning. "You won't come that close to your finish more'n once more, kid. Never hopped a train before, King?"

It amazed Billy English that the brakeman should know his companion, but when the fellow went on, The King took much credit to himself for this fact.

"They all know old King Charlie," he said, leaning back on his elbows. "They all know me, eh, Billy? Took years to get as well known as I am along this road. Years and years and years! Some day maybe you'll have as big a rep. Would you like that?"

"Sort of," said Billy without enthusiasm. "I dunno but I could get along without it, though."

The older man cast a glance at him and decided that he must continually use caution in his words to the youth.

"Look yonder," he said, by way of diverting attention. "Look at the way we're flying into the west and into the sunset, Billy. I guess that this beats riding a hoss, eh?"

Billy English shook his head. "It's just different," he declared. "These planks under you may be going fast, but they ain't thinking and feeling the same's you are thinking and feeling. These planks can go faster, but they ain't a hoss, sir. Nope!"

The King shrugged his shoulders. This absurd notion must be extracted from the mind of the boy when there was time for it. In the meanwhile, he looked about him and placidly regarded the flitting of the miles. All was going so easily, so swimmingly, as compared with the footsore miles of the desert, that it seemed an easy thing to tell the prodigious lie toward which he had been drifting ever since he had heard how Billy English was found in Carterville.

"Billy," he said, "what do you remember about your father?"

"Nothing much," said Billy. "You see, I was only four when — Well, the gent that I guess must of been my father was just sort of tall. But I ain't a bit sure about anything; nothing about him, that is. I remember my mother; that's all."

"What you remember about her?"

"Things I don't talk about," said the boy with a blending of dignity and sadness that moved the hardened tramp in spite of himself. "Things," he added, "that I couldn't talk about."

Plainly, then, his past was a mist. That was all The King wanted to know.

"Would you like," he said, "to know more about your father?"

"Would I like to go to heaven?" said the boy, trembling with sudden eagerness. Then he whirled on The King and gripped him.

"You knew him," he said, "or you know him now. He — he's still alive. He's sent you to find me! Is that why you followed me down the road? But why —"

"Listen," said The King, quivering with an emotion which was real, though it was not at all what it seemed to be. "When you met up with me, did you feel anything queer, Billy?"

"I dunno. Why?"

"I'll ask you a question right back. Why are you here?"

"Because — because I had a fight with Shaw."

"That any reason for you to swipe a ride on a train like this?"

"You told me to —"

He stopped short.

"That's it, Billy. I told you to. And why did you do what I told you to?"

Billy English frowned heavily. "What are you driving at?" he asked.

"When you first seen me," said King Charlie, playing his cards with care and swiftness combined for this great stake, "why was it that you started right in doing what I told you to do — and why was it that I was the only one on the field that knowed really just how you was feeling underneath your smile?"

Billy, who had regained some of his color, now lost it again.

"D'you mean — I don't foller you, I guess!"

"You do, but you won't let yourself. Look hard at me, Billy. Look me straight in the eye!"

The boy obeyed.

"Don't you recognize nothing — don't you feel nothing?" cried King Charlie, throwing into the voice all the feeling he could, and in his present state of mind that was not difficult. "Look hard at me, Billy, while I tell you my right name. I'm Charles English!"

Billy English winced and gaped at his companion.

"You mean —"

"Don't you see," cried the tramp, "that that's why I'd walked across the desert to find you? It was an instinct leading me back toward the place. And then I seen you on the field riding the hoss and something jumped in me: 'It's him!' says I to myself. 'No, he's dead eleven black years ago,' says myself to me. Then I ask about you, and they tell me how you come in from the railroad tracks ten or eleven years ago saying that you was four years old, and that your name was Billy English. When I heard that name, my head started spinning. I near went out cold. I kept telling myself that it couldn't be true!"

While he spoke, The King watched the boy's face shrewdly, and he saw that Billy was moved past incredulity, and had been swept into the tide of the narrative.

"And then," went on The King, "I said to myself: 'Can I show myself to him? Can I let him see me the way I am — without a home — without money — with nothing but my self-respect left to me — that and my freedom which they couldn't take away from me? Can I show myself to him the way I am, and take him away from a good home, maybe?' I says. And then I start to find out, and pretty soon I know that you ain't got a good home at all. No, because an old skinflint that's working your hands to the bone has you. And then I says, 'I'll go and see him and try if he likes to live this life with me — of freedom that can't be bought!' And so, Billy, here we are; after eleven years you and your father are joined together on the train — on the same tracks where we lost each other eleven years before!"

He felt that his speech had trailed off into a most ridiculously unemphatic conclusion, and he would not have been at all surprised had Billy English burst into ringing laughter and pointed a finger of derision at him. But too many strange things had happened to poor Billy that day. They had

56

broken down the barriers of his caution, and now he had no power to stand back and criticize what he heard.

For a moment of bitter suspense he threw back his head and stared into the eyes of King Charlie, and then he caught the hands of the rascal in a strong grip.

"Good Lord!" he said. "How I've dreamed about this — how I've plumb ached for it!"

CHAPTER VIII

IN THE JUNGLE

Into such a happy delirium had Billy English fallen that it was easy for The King to answer the babel of questions which now poured out on him.

The story he told was one which he had only loosely sketched to himself before, and which he now told with as little detail as possible, filling it in as he went along. He had been, he said, a prosperous man, happy with his wife and his child, until the tragedy overtook them. That tragedy occurred when little Billy disappeared from the train in which his wife was traveling. The train had slowed at a water tank, and Billy had gone back to the platform, to look out. There he must have climbed down; when the conductor came inside and shut up the platform again, Billy must have been left on the ground outside.

All this was what they guessed later, and this was what must have happened; but in the meantime, Mrs. English had fallen asleep, and it was a matter of several hours before she wakened and missed the boy. When he left her, she could not say, and the train had made a dozen stops during the time she slept.

There was nothing for it but to advertise in the papers and send inquiries back to every station along the line. But since there was no station or station agent at the tank where Billy had really escaped, no search was made into the surrounding country. That was the only manner in which he could explain the failure to find Billy.

In the meantime, Mrs. English grew sick with anxiety; a short time afterward she sank under a slight malady and died. He himself would not give up the search, but, abandoning his drygoods business in St. Louis, he had taken to the road in search for the boy until, examining into the particulars of the run of the train on that division on the night of Billy's disappearance, he learned what had not been previously reported through the negligence of the train crew — that when the train pulled into the next town it was found that under the train there were crimson stains and evidences that some one had been crushed on the track. It was simply held that some tramp had fallen from the rods, and no more attention was paid to the matter; but The King was convinced that this was the fate of his son.

After this he made a futile effort to run his business, but all went wrong; and when his business failed completely he took to the road again, drifting here and there, the life of a vagrant, with the power of society directed all against him. And so he had fought on, reckless as to how he lived, sent again and again to prison, usually for crimes which he had not committed, until at length he had come to be what the boy beheld him.

He painted the picture as black as possible, for now he was attributing all his guilt indirectly to the disappearance of Billy; he was placing the burden deftly on the shoulders of the boy; and, though Billy winced and shrank, it was plain that he accepted the tale as gospel truth.

Darkness, in the meantime, had fallen, and The King was profoundly grateful to nature for veiling his face from the eyes of the boy as he concluded his invention.

After that a long silence fell between them, and in the end he felt the hand of the boy fall reverently and affectionately on his shoulder. There was little honesty or generosity left in the heart of The King, but at this touch he came close indeed to recanting his lie and telling Billy English that it was all a jest. But his tongue cleaved to the roof of his mouth when he attempted to speak, and the truth remained unspoken.

Then he listened to Billy's account of his own uneventful, work-tormented life, with all the story of his ambitions and hopes worked in toward the end. In conclusion they spoke of the future, and in this the "father" took the guiding hand. They would settle down to an honest and industrious life very soon, and in the meantime it would be necessary for The King to complete one or two small affairs. He would, in short, have to mingle for a while with gentlemen of his own ilk along the road, and Billy must come with him.

Among the "jungles," he told Billy, they must

never refer to each other as father and son. For a thousand reasons it would be better simply to treat each other as friends.

Their narratives and these plannings for the future occupied the time until they approached the swirling and scattered lights, far ahead, of a small town; and when the freight took a siding here, the tramp and Billy English swung down to the ground, and King Charlie led the way to the far side of the village.

Weary from the long day and the hard work which he had crowded into part of it, exhausted by all the strange things that had happened to him, Billy English stumbled along behind the tall man who walked with such an elastic, untiring step — the man whom he was hereafter to think of as father.

Strangely conflicting emotions swayed in the boy's heart as he walked. Vagabond and disreputable in many ways he knew that man to be; and besides, that suspicion which most honest folk feel even subconsciously for the evaders of the law, was still like a shadow in the back of his brain.

Yet he went on. He was far too tired to think out the tangled problem at this time of night. A fire now gleamed and winked afar off among the trees, momentarily growing in size and distinctness, until they broke into a small glade. Billy English beheld for the first time in his life a tramp jungle where the wanderers of the earth gather, to cook their stews, brew their coffee, made of ten-times boiled coffee grounds, perhaps, and

61

wash their clothes — if they be nice in their habits — and then exchange tales with what company they may find in the resort.

On this night the fire was surrounded by a goodly assembly. A jail in a town some fifty miles away had just disgorged a half dozen vagrants who, having been arrested on the same day, were turned loose on the same day, and had come to the conclusion of their first day's journey after receiving liberty together.

These, having received a few dollars for their work for the county on being liberated, were now flush; they had come to the jungle laden with dainties dear to the heart of a hobo. Canned tomatoes, onions, potatoes, and chickens they had contributed to the contents of the enormous stew which now simmered in a big wash boiler, and over which stood the eldest and most trusted cook of the six, stirring the mulligan from time to time with a long stick, one end of which had been whittled clean. In the meantime, the others of the company, men of all ages from the lean twenties to the grizzled fifties, sat around in a semicircle hugging their knees and with their heads thrown back while, like so many wolves, they inhaled the aroma of the coming feast.

However, they were not the only claimants of the camp fire. On the other side of the blaze were three worn and tattered veterans of the road which had no ending. Unshaven for days, and uninterested in shaving, dressed in patched odds and ends of clothes, these blowed-in-the-glass stiffs, permanent and unchangeable tramps, lounged at their ease, making themselves as comfortable as possible, and attempting to show no interest in the mulligan, of which they had not the money to buy a share, though they writhed as in pain when the changeable wind on occasion wafted the fragrance of the stew toward them.

The sight of these mangy rascals made Billy English shiver with aversion and, turning his glance sharply to one side, he looked into the face of the last member of the camp-fire party. This was a wide-shouldered man who lay flat on his back, with the heel of one foot based on the toe of the other, puffing at a half-finished cigar, with his hat drawn deep over his eyes. His clothes were of far better make than those of any other person in the glade, and his whole appearance was such that he might have passed easy muster as a respectable member of society on a city street.

Toward him The King also had now turned his gaze, and the first sight of the man who lay prone caused him to start.

"Colytt!" he said. "By the Lord, it's Colytt! Ain't that luck for once in a year?"

So saying, he stepped out from the shadow of the trees where he had until this moment lingered; striding to the man he had termed Colytt, he kicked the uppermost foot of the latter sharply.

The result was as surprising as the release of a tightly coiled watch spring. Colytt came to his feet with a leap and showed a dark, regular-featured face, now scowling with malignance. His hand was back to strike when he recognized the smiling face of Charlie.

It required a moment for him to let the snarl relax from his lips, and then with a shamefaced smile he extended his hand.

"Hello, King," he said. "Blowed if you didn't give me a start. Hey, bos! Here's The King. Here's King Charlie!"

That announcement operated like magic upon the rest of the tramps, who came to their feet of one accord and sent a clamor toward the celebrity. In another moment he was among them, and they were busy shaking his hand. Only the three dyed-in-the-wool veterans made no move to approach him. He went around the fire and stood over them, his hand extended, and Billy English shuddered to see his father meet such creatures on their own level.

"Chicago Lou!" cried The King. "And here's old Whitey from York. Blowed if it ain't good to lay eyes on you, boys!"

At that signal, as though they had been holding back, not sure that recognition would be welcome to him, they started up and took his hand one by one, at the same time glancing proudly toward the others on the far side of the fire.

"Have you had chuck yet?" asked The King.

They averred that they had not, and he stepped to the wash boiler and glanced at the contents.

"Enough for a dozen," he declared. "I'll pay for your share to-night. Hey, Billy!"

Billy English followed slowly into the firelight

and stood frowning on all sides.

"Here you are, pals," said The King. "I want to make you known to a side-stepper of mine — Billy English!"

CHAPTER IX

GULLIBLE YOUTH

THAT was the introduction of Billy to this class of men. He shook hands with them hesitantly, feeling that he must be at least as friendly toward them as his father was. But inside him something revolted against them. They, for their part, were entirely cordial. The youngster had not that rat-look which they were accustomed to see in youthful recruits to their order, but if King Charlie introduced the lad he must be all right.

So they made Billy welcome; they gave him a good seat by the fire, and furnished him a large and steaming portion of mulligan and "punk" — bread — in a big tomato can. He dipped into the provender cautiously, for the can had not seemed entirely clean, and the mulligan appeared to contain every variety of food of which he could think.

Everything goes into mulligan: pieces of stale bread, tomatoes, potatoes, vegetables of any kind, peppers, marrow-bones, meat of any sort chopped up, pepper and salt in reasonable quantities. But a vast hunger urged him to taste the stew, and he found it delectable beyond words. It is, in fact, the best possible way to prepare an appetizing ration out of cheap materials.

66

About him he heard slang which he could hardly follow, so thick was it, and so strange were the words to him. When he heard one ragged gentleman, for instance, speak of "getting a stretch for soaking an elbow," it did not dawn on the untutored brain of Billy that the man was simply saying that he had been sentenced to a year's imprisonment for beating a detective. Nor did he gather the meaning when he learned that another man had "got an anchor when he was due to go up Salt Creek," but later on Billy, having enjoyed the fare, found those who had cooked it better fellows than he had at first suspected.

When they had eaten, the tone of their conversation changed — grew considerably heightened — and as they told yarns, disputed, jested with growing abandon, Billy noticed that The King and the wide-shouldered gentleman had drawn apart and were conversing softly together.

The purport of their conversation was somewhat as follows:

"Where'd you pick up the kid?" asked Colytt. "He don't look the right kind, King."

"He ain't the right kind, my boy," said the older man. "Matter of fact, he ain't the right kind at all. But if he's handled with gloves he may turn out to be worth ten times as much as one of the right kind. Ever hear of any of the right kind showing any gratitude to them that taught 'em everything they knew, or ever hear of 'em staying around and helping when the gents that done the teaching go down on their luck? No, you never heard nothing like that. But this is a clean-bred 'un, Colytt, as they say on the Blue Grass. He'll act different if I can keep a hold on him and learn him something."

Colytt cocked his big, ugly head to one side. "You was always a smooth one, King," he said. "Well, go ahead with the kid, and I wish you luck. But I tell you this to start with: You can't change the color of a cat."

"Croak if you want to," said The King, "but sit up and watch results when I'm through."

That prodigious lie about the fatherhood of the boy he dared not communicate to even so hardy a character as Colytt.

"What's on now?" The King asked. "Working up a plant?"

"Got a plant all laid out," said Colytt mournfully, "but I got nobody to work it with me."

"What's the matter with me?" asked The King.

Colytt smiled. "You with the shakes?" he said. "No hope, pardner. You'd be meaning well in the thick of it, if something went wrong, but you might not be no good to me or yourself. You know that."

The King snapped his teeth together.

"Maybe not," he said, "but what about the kid?"

"Too young. You'd ought to know that."

"Why?"

"This work I got planned is risky stuff, King. If it comes to a pinch I got to have somebody along that I'll be sure has the nerve to shoot and shoot straight."

"Listen me, bo. I picked this kid up at a hoss

68

breaking contest that he lost because he'd absorbed all the punch that there was in the hoss, and the other gent was just rocked in a cradle. And then, I tried this boy out with his gat. I threw a can in the air — a little oyster can half as big as your fist. I chucked it high and far, and told him to blaze away when it started dropping. His draw was as pretty as a picture, and he drilled that can clean through the center before it had a chance to kiss the dust. How does that sound to you, Colytt?"

So excited had Colytt become during the recital that, as he was sitting cross-legged, he rocked far forward until his knees pressed against the ground. "That's as neat as anything I ever heard tell about even you, King."

"Maybe. But how does he sound to you now, Colytt?"

Colytt looked critically toward the boy, and The King sat back to wait. Colytt had been a safe blower in the East before that part of the country became too hot for him, and he had moved West to become one of those cold-nerved adventurers who roamed up and down the length and the breadth of the mountain desert, striking their blows here and there, and escaping with their loot as best they could, depending for their safety upon the speed and endurance of their horses, the knowledge of the country which they studied until every mile of it was mapped in their memories, and their friends among the small ranchers, nesters, and trappers, whom they cultivated with small donations of money when they were flush.

In spite of all that they could do, their lives were a continual and desperate hazard, as their class title "long riders" signified. Colytt was a type of them, if there could be a type. Fierce, fearless, incapable of fatigue, cunning as a wolverene, and as strong, never fighting save when it was absolutely necessary, and then always fighting to kill, he had lived perhaps seven years on the ranges; and into that space of time he had crammed the deeds of seven wicked lifetimes. It was for these reasons that the evil mind of The King hung in suspense as he waited for Colytt to pronounce judgment.

"He looks good to me," said Colytt at length, in his deep voice. "He looks good. He ain't one of those talky kids. He ain't told them bums a thing about himself. But how could you persuade a clean-set kid like that to go busting peters, King?"

"There's ways of doing everything," said The King. "I'll do the persuading. But tell me what your lay is."

"There's a runt of a bank down at Yorkville, a little town over the hill. It's easy to get the safe, but it ain't going to be any too easy to get out of town after we start the racket. They's been a couple of stick-ups around there."

"Could we get hosses?"

"Sure. I got a friend out 'long the way, here. He's got a couple of good skates. I got a couple myself over behind the bushes yonder. You go talk to the kid, will you?"

The King accordingly went to Billy English, who was nodding in the heat of the fire, and only half hearing what the hobos around him said. The King called him away, and put his point with a directness that should be convincing, if anything were.

"Billy," he said, "you seen me talking to Colytt?"

The boy nodded.

"He's been telling me about some dirty work that a bank down in Yorkville done a rancher friend of his. Seems that this bank got his pal into a close corner with a mortgage, and then closed in on him and grabbed everything he had. Understand?"

"Not quite," said Billy. "But —"

"They do terrible things to a gent that has a mortgage agin' him," said The King sadly. "I know, because it's been done to me. In this case they just cleaned the poor fellow out of house and home and put his wife and five kiddies out from under a roof — three little girls and two curly-headed boys. Ain't that a rotten thing to hear, Billy?"

Billy clicked his teeth. "Something had sure ought to be done about it," he snapped out.

"That's what Colytt has been thinking," said The King. "That's what made him so darned thoughtful and quiet when we first seen him here. He was wondering how he could help that friend of his — understand?"

"He must be a good man," said simple Billy English with warmth. "He must be a fine sort of a gent, sir. I didn't think he was when I first looked at him."

That "sir" rang to the very heart of the old rascal as he watched the boy, and once again, for the hundredth time, he wavered in his purpose. But, no; this youthful Billy English must serve as The King's meal ticket when the latter grew old.

"But what can he do?" asked Billy.

"He's going to get that money back for his friend," said The King sternly. "He's going down and blow open the safe that the money is kept in, and take as much as belongs to his friend and then get away and —"

"But that —" gasped out Billy. "What would happen if he was caught breaking into the bank?"

"Penitentiary," said The King darkly. "Think what he's risking for his friend!"

Billy caught his breath again. "All alone?" he asked.

"No, Billy. I'm going to go along and do what little I can, though I'm not much account in such affairs!"

The boy caught his arm. "Could I go along and do what I can? D'you think he'd trust me that far?"

It was so ridiculously easy that The King could have laughed aloud, had he not been a trifle concerned to see the boy so gullible. But, after all, he decided that it was not so strange, considering the fact that Billy English felt that his own father was telling him these things.

"I dunno," said The King with great gravity. "We'll go back and ask him if you can come along."

CHAPTER X

BILLY IS AMUSED

TWENTY minutes later, with Colytt on one horse
and Billy English on the other — for The King
vowed he'd rather walk than ride, at least for a
short distance — they proceeded away from the
jungle at a brisk walk for The King; the horses,
from time to time swung into a jogging trot to
keep up with the swing of those long legs.

Considering the gravity of the work before them,
there was astonishingly little talk, it seemed to
Billy. The main theme of conversation was introduced by The King after they had been going for
only a short distance, and it was a strange topic
to start on such a trip, keeping in mind their destination.

He held forth at length, in the first place, upon
the difficulty of such a thing as a bank robbery,
and the great probability that the robbers, if they
showed the slightest weakness, would fall a prey
to the vigorous pursuit, even if they were so lucky
as to get away from the town itself. Many a man
had been so captured, whereas those bandits who
rushed boldly upon a town, galloped to their selected bank, blew open the safe, or called on the
cashier for the money and then rode off shooting

74

in all directions — these men went safe time and again.

The inference was plain — that this was the preferable method. Unfortunately they did not have enough men to act in this manner. He went on to tell what happened to those who were captured. Usually they were instantly hanged to the nearest trees by the infuriated townsfolk; or, if they did not act with such immediate violence, a destiny even more terrible awaited the robber. He was sent off to prison, and there he was treated with particular brutality. Bread and water became his portion, and he was made to labor all day, while at night he slept in a dark cell, to which little air entered. His imprisonment was for a term of twenty-five or thirty years, it appeared, according to The King.

"But," cried poor Billy English, "I heard about a gent taken for bank robbery, that was pardoned after he'd been in only five years. I read about that in the papers."

"You read lots of queerer things than that in the papers," said The King wisely. "Besides, a couple of exceptions only go to prove the rule. Am I right, Colytt?"

There was a grunt from Colytt, and Billy fell into a brown study which led him to exactly the conclusion that The King wished to carry him to, namely: That, rather than be captured in the robbery of a bank, it was far preferable to be killed, and obviously, therefore, it was better to shoot to kill in turn. With all his might poor Billy wished that the unnamed friend of Colytt had been served in some other manner, but he dared not ask questions, and he was ashamed to show the white feather.

But when the crisis came, what would he do in case there were a close pursuit? Would he shoot to kill rather than risk the miserable fate of prison or the shameful death on the end of a rope hanging from the nearest tree?

In this dire dilemma he felt his opinion sway back and forth. To hang or die in prison was horrible; to kill in self-defense was yet more horrible; and most shameful of all was it to draw out of an enterprise in which his own father adventured so fearlessly!

They reached a house, at the door of which Colytt knocked and held consultation with the man who answered the summons, lantern in hand. Then he went out to a small shed behind the house, saddled a horse which he found there, and returned, leading this to The King. So, all three mounted, they now scurried ahead at a more rapid pace, and The King swung in beside Billy English for a time and drew for him the long and quiet content of the life that was to be theirs, once this disagreeable and necessary job of the night should be finished. He, The King, would have new courage to carve out an honest and honorable career, he avowed, now that he had his boy again.

He proved his good spirits by breaking into a ringing song a moment later, which was harshly cut short by the voice of Colytt.

"Stop that noise, will you?" cried the yegg. "You think I want to have everybody in the county know that we're on the road to-night?"

The King made no protest, but stopped singing; and as he did so they came over the top of a hill and in sight of a town sprawled out in a long, loose chain of lights, the scattering nature of which was ample indication that the majority of the people in Yorkville were asleep. Billy English vaguely and wretchedly traced the outline of the town. It was like Carterville, grouped entirely around one long street or road.

Orders were issued briefly by Colytt on the way down the hill. There was one watchman on guard, but he had previously "fixed" that watchman, and as soon as he appeared and gave the signal, the watchman would receive a hurry call to go on some pressing errand down the street, for the bank was not the only place he watched.

The raiders' chief anxiety was to guard against chance passers-by, for the windows of the bank were glass, the safe was mortally near the front of the building, and it was very possible that any one who came by might see the shadow of Colytt through that uncurtained window.

The King was to stay at the rear of the bank, therefore, to watch for any one who might come in that direction, which some official of the bank might possibly do to finish up some work since it was not much more than ten thirty.

The main danger would be guarded against by Billy English in front of the bank, where he was to take his stand by the side of his horse, and, having first spent some time fumbling at his reins, which he could claim had come unbraided should any one approach, he could then go on to examine the hoofs as though it had picked up a pebble, and in this fashion kill the time until the explosion were heard.

In that case, he was to swing into the saddle and rein his horse between the bank and the next building, and so guard the rear and open fire on all who came near, until the whistle of the two in the rear of the bank announced that Colytt was clear with the loot. In the meantime, should some one come down the street, Billy was to commence whistling "Auld Lang Syne," and Colytt would desist in his work or keep safely out of view until the danger passed.

Fifteen minutes later Billy found himself at the designated post, standing at the side of his horse and working foolishly, without purpose, at his reins. But the village street was perfectly dark, and no one came in view through what seemed an eternity, though all the time he could see forms pass and repass across the lighted shade of a window in a house not fifty yards away.

Every moment he expected to hear the explosion, though as a matter of fact Colytt would need far more time. But seconds dragged past like minutes with Billy.

Now came a new alarm and added danger. The night, which had been thick as a fog in the beginning, now rapidly thinned away so that he could look the length of the street; and next he saw a slowly ascending fire drift up through the trees on a distant hill and take shape at the top as a yellow moon appeared at the full!

The devil was indeed in it to take away the kindly dark which had shielded them!

Here, a moment later, came a singing fellow who sauntered idly down the street, not hurrying like a man who wishes to get somewhere, but ambling on as though he were merely out to enjoy the night. The heart of Billy climbed into his throat.

Busily he began prodding at the hoof of his horse when he had lifted the leg. He was aware that the stranger had paused, and, turning to the other side of the horse with a muffled "Hello," he picked up that hoof in turn and began to examine it.

But the stranger did not pass on. He stayed.

"What's wrong?" he asked.

Billy turned and faced a strongly built man of perhaps thirty-five, a solid form, as suggestive of muscular power as the form of Colytt himself.

"Picked up a pebble, I guess," said Billy. "He started limping on me, so I got off to take a look."

The other chuckled.

"Well," he said, "you ain't much of a hand with hosses, son, if you can't tell which foot a hoss is limping on. Where'd you come from?"

He dropped a hand carelessly on the top of the nearest post of the hitching rack. Sweat rolled out on the forehead of Billy English, though the night was cold. Suppose that this talkative fool were to stay here until the explosion went off? At his side he wore a big forty-five in a most workmanlike fashion, low on his thigh, and if ever a man looked the part of an alert fighter, this was he. When he heard that noise, things would begin to happen in this street, and they would happen with great precision.

Would this fellow shoot him down, or was he doomed to shoot down the stranger?

"Where'd you come from?" repeated the other, more aggressively. "Didn't you hear me, kid?"

"Over yonder," said Billy, waving his hand vaguely.

"What's that mean? Troyton?"

"Yep; beyond Troyton."

"You mean on the other side of the river, eh?"

"That's right."

The other laughed softly. "There ain't any river beyond Troyton, kid. Now tell me: What're you doing here?"

Billy leaned back against the shoulder of the horse.

He was very sick and cold in the pit of the stomach.

"I dunno what you mean," he murmured.

"Don't you?" said the other. "Look here, son, you run away from home to join the gold rush up in —"

The sentence was split away to nothing by a dull and muffled sound like the dropping of an immensely heavy weight, wrapped in thick mufflings, upon an immensely strong floor. The big man turned like a flash toward the bank.

"By thunder!" he cried as the meaning dawned on him, and his gun whipped from its holster.

He was late, however, far too late, for the practiced hand of Billy had automatically slipped out his gun the instant he heard the explosion; and now his finger curled around the trigger and held the life of the stranger in the balance.

The latter whirled — and Billy stepped in with the sudden energy of a desperate man and struck with the long, heavy barrel of the gun. The blow landed squarely along the head of the other, and he toppled back into the thick dust, sending a bullet at the sky.

Over him leaned Billy. Had he killed the man? No, there was life in that sturdy body, though Billy could have sworn that he had felt the skull sag under the blow.

But the explosion of the gun had roused a score of human echoes near by. Doors banged, and voices rang out upon porches. Men began calling to one another until one dominant throat shouted: "The bank — look yonder! Hey, there, who are you?"

Billy was already swinging into the saddle. He did not wait to reply, but, leaving the dark, sprawled figure against the white of the moonlit dust behind him — a damning accusation — he spurred his horse around the corner of the bank.

Two bullets chipped the bricks as he whirled to safety, and voices roared directions as to how they should cut off his retreat, but that retreat was not the immediate object in the eyes of Billy.

Panic had him by the throat, but still he remembered the orders of The King.

Under the shelter of the wall of the bank he whirled his horse around, and, riding back to the verge of the street, he fired — into the air at such an angle that he could not strike any one — up, down, and across — with the result that the pursuers, who had been rushing out, guns in hand, to do battle, now scattered for shelter with yells, only sending a desultory fire behind them as they gave way.

At the same moment there was a sharp whistle, immediately broken off and reënforced with curses, from the rear of the bank, and Billy twitched his neat-footed horse around and spurred for safety.

He had not too much time. They were swarming like hornets behind him, and bullets were smashing against the wall of the bank from a dozen different directions. He brought the horse swerving into the open stretch behind the bank, and saw two dark forms darting away across the open fields.

After these he loosed his rein and came rapidly upon them. At the edge of a small grove of scrub oak he caught up with them, but they gave him neither glance nor word until they had topped the next rise. From that point of vantage, they looked down upon the moonlit plain and saw the posse streaming in pursuit.

Then: "Cuss all the luck this side of Hades!" roared Colytt.

"You didn't have time enough," said Billy. "I

guess I didn't give you time enough to get what you wanted."

"You? Time enough? Good Lord, you gave me time enough to carry the whole bank away; you done noble, kid! The old King, there, couldn't have bested what you done in his palmiest days; but the safe" — here a torrid explosion of oaths followed — "was double! Me, like a fool — I thought it was just a tin can; but inside that rusty old piece of junk they was a brand-new outfit!"

All that danger, and not a cent had been taken! But Billy English, for some strange reason, merely tilted back his head and broke into shrill, musical laughter while they turned the heads of their horses to the left and glided away under cover of the hills.

CHAPTER XI

SCARED AT A THOUGHT

THE slanting, warm sunshine falling on the face of The King the next morning wakened him. He shifted himself slowly to one side along the floor of the shanty to which he and Billy English and Colytt had come at the end of their flight, so far from any sign of pursuit that they had decided to risk sleeping here.

For a time, as the sunshine dropped in on the rest of his body, he lay luxuriating in the warmth which thawed the night chill out of his limbs, and which, it seemed, was likewise thawing his mind and permitting the disastrous events of the evening before to filter into his recollection.

It was very bad, in one respect, and very good in another. It was bad in that the stroke had fallen and had not brought to them the rich returns with which he had promised himself to corrupt the mind of the boy forever. With gold he would buy him to the easy life of yegg and long rider. It was very good, however, in that the youngster had shown such dauntless grit.

Yes, Billy English certainly had the nerve for the work, the coolness and the address. To be sure, he had seemed a little shaky on the way into Yorkville, but the important thing was that he had stood watch dauntlessly while the deft Colytt was running the mold of soft soap around the door of the safe. He had stood guard, and he had fought for the general good of the three in the time of need.

So much did the thought of this warm the heart of The King that he closed his eyes again and lay for a long time dreaming of the good time to come when the power of this boy, trained by his own skill and the brain of Colytt, would begin to crack safes. Then they would live on the fat of the land indeed! What a series of hauls it would be!

He could no longer contain himself, so great had grown his self-content. He sat up. There lay Colytt, his face buried in his arms, breathing heavily. But Billy was gone. No doubt he was busy somewhere in that bright sunshine, fishing for trout in the stream they had heard running the night before.

"Colytt!" he called.

Colytt opened one eye.

"It's morning."

"I don't care if it's night. We missed the loot and —"

"Hush up — easy! Don't let the kid hear you talk none too frequent about loot. We're doing all this for the good of your friend, you know."

"Cuss my friend," replied Colytt, but nevertheless he softened his voice as he sat up. He rubbed the sleep out of his eyes, and then turned his ugly face toward The King. "A game kid, that. He sure is the grit, King!"

85

"Ain't he? I told you I could pick 'em!"

"And he said he was game to stay with us and try again, didn't he?"

"That's right, I'd almost forgotten about that Colytt!"

"A good kid, I say. I'll have to take him in hand and begin teaching him things. He'll take to it like a duck to water. Hello, what's that?"

A piece of wrapping paper fluttered from the wall, to which it was attached with a splinter.

"Covered with writing," said Colytt, and he scooped the paper from the wall, started to read, and then roared: "He's gone!"

The King, with a cry that was half groan, half whine, leaped up, caught the paper, and read aloud in his turn:

"DEAR KING CHARLIE AND COLYTT: I hate to sneak off like this in the middle of the night, but I got to do it. This is why. You two are going to get some money to help a friend, which is all very fine and right. But you're going to get it by busting into the bank. Well, I can't stand it.

"I'll tell you why. When I was on guard in the front of the bank last night, I was plumb scared to start with, but after a while I began to get over it. Then came the explosion and the guns going off all around me, and I thought that I ought to be scared to within an inch of my life, but I wasn't.

"Matter of fact, I liked it. That sounds

86

queer, but it's true. It was more fun than anything I've ever done in my whole life!"

The King paused.
"Can you beat that?" muttered Colytt.
"You can't," said The King, and continued at once with the reading:

"When we got away I felt like singing. So when we reached the shack, and you two went to sleep right away, I couldn't sleep. I lay awake seeing everything all over again, and I wanted to go right down and do it once more.

"Well, after a while I saw where that was leading to: If I didn't watch out, I'd be doing things like that, not to help out anybody that had been treated bad and lost money, but simply to get the excitement again.

"That thought scared me, and I saw what I had to do. I had to get away before you woke up, because when you woke up, we'd go and try this thing again. And if I did it once more I'd get a regular hunger for it fixed in me. That's why I'm sneaking off this way all quiet.

"I'd sure like to see you both again. King, if you'll drop around to Carterville inside a year, say just a year from to-day, I'll be there to meet you, but I sure can't trust myself now. I got to try myself out!"

Here the letter ended with the postscript:

"I ain't taking a hoss. I'm going to go over to the railroad and start traveling the way you showed me, King. I'm aiming back for hosses and cows. That's where I belong."

The King lowered the paper, dazed, and he barely heard the torrid curses of Colytt.

"I thought you knowed this kid?" cried Colytt. "I thought you knowed what he'd do? I thought he'd stay with you?"

"Don't talk to me," said The King.

"He'll come back, though," said Colytt.

"Not for a year," said The King sadly. "Not for a whole year. And then, when he does come back, I won't have no hold on him. He'll know all the truth about me then. Why, right now he thinks that I'm an honest man, or pretty near honest. And — he thinks a lot of other things about me! A year from now he'd laugh in my face!"

"Well," said Colytt, "don't take it so hard. He was your insurance against old age, but you'll get along, anyway. You got the brains to get along."

"Brains don't give you lots of things."

"What?"

"Well, a family, for instance — a son!"

"What're you talking about?" cried Colytt.

"Nothing!" sighed The King.

CHAPTER XII

ONE YEAR LATER

WITH dolorous eye King Charlie looked above the trees and marked where the bald, bare mountains shot up against the moonlit sky. To him this cattle country of the Western mountains represented all that was gloomily forbidding. He could see no reason why any man — ay, or any creatures other than vipers and Gila monsters and starveling coyotes — should wish to remain in its precincts.

Only a quest of the most vital importance, a need which had haunted him during the past year, made him return. Now he sat in what he told himself would prove the last comfortable jungle between that point and the coast. In between there was a vast expanse of hardy country and scarcely less hardy towns.

Instead of hobos ranging swiftly hither and yon on the railroads, there were dauntless long riders, as they were called, which simply meant men who covered great distances in the saddle, striking here and there at widely separated points just as traveling yeggs will do, with this difference: That the yegg melts back into the obscurity of the drift life of the railroads and finds safety in swiftly stirring numbers, whereas the long rider drops back into

89

the wide silence of the desert and finds safety in the solitude.

King Charlie looked back, with a shiver of apprehension, to the fire where the mulligan had been cooked. It had been a very good mulligan. The tramps who had ventured into this outlying territory were one and all good rustlers, able to "throw their feet" — collect supplies — with the best. Most of them were, like Charlie, tramp royals, blowed-in-the-glass stiffs who disdained to carry a roll of bedding or to lift a hand in honest labor at any time. They had fixed this jungle for the night so that it represented the maximum of comfort.

A steady wind came piercingly out of the north, weaving through the shrubbery and cutting through the stoutest clothes like knife points through soft butter. Against it the fellowship, under the direction of King Charlie — who, of course, never did more than direct — had erected a barrier of dead branches broken from the trees or picked up from the ground, and upon this framework, in turn, they built a thick thatching of shrubs, whose more dense foliage, thus arranged in several layers, sufficed to turn the wind and leave them comfortable behind their shield. The fire had then been built, and in a great wash boiler the stew was made for a dozen men, and each of the dozen — except King Charlie again — had contributed his share. What The King did was to pay for all he ate.

Listening to the talk which was going on around

him, The King found that his companions were laying plans to defend one of their number from danger of attack by another hobo called "The Kid." He who was threatened was a formidable fellow, lank jawed, lank limbed, with the ferocity of a mink in his little reddish eyes. But he sat with his great hands locked around his knees and drank in with insatiable greed the assurances of his comrades that they would stand by him if The Kid should come. One had a knife handy to tickle the ribs of The Kid. Another had a trusty club. Another, in case of final need, would draw his gat and pump a shower of lead into The Kid's vitals.

"But who," interrupted King Charlie, turning his handsome though rather harsh-featured face toward the rest, "is The Kid? What's the rest of his monica? Denver Kid, or The Blondy Kid from Chi — what's his whole monica, bos?"

"Don't you know The Kid?" they responded in chorus.

"Sure. I know a thousand kids," answered King Charlie. "But what about this one? What's his particular label?"

All eyes turned to the lanky man who had been receiving the promises of immunity from the terrible Kid.

"There's just one and only one Kid," said Skinny. "That's why they didn't hang another monica on him. He hasn't been on the road very long. He plays the blind baggage and the rods, some; but mostly he hangs right close to the moun-

91

tains and does his traveling by hossback. Among the long riders he's a big gun. Some say he ain't been on the road more'n a year, and that he ain't more'n sixteen right now, though he looks three years older. But he's all boiled down wild cat, you see, King? He's spent six months of his year in the pen, and there he got hardened up and learned a whole pile. When he come out, he started to use what he'd learned. Anything from train stick-up to cracking a peter is nuts for him. He's a genius, that's what he is; and if it wasn't for the fact that he'll be dead before he's twenty, he'd be a credit to anybody's bringing up."

"What was the bust between you and The Kid, Skinny?" asked King Charlie.

"I was batty with moonshine, and I rolled a pal of his for a goal," said Skinny sadly. "We had a mix-up on top of a train, and his pal done a tumble off the top. He didn't die, but he got both legs busted, and now The Kid is paying his doctor bills. Also he's out to get me; but the boys will give him his hands full, the young devil!"

"Does he fight fair?" asked The King.

"Is a tornado fair?" growled Skinny in response. "You see it coming, but that doesn't let you know how to keep it from tearing the roof off your house, does it?"

When an hour had gone by, the exciting topic of The Kid was quite forgotten. It was recalled again by a sharp scuffle of rising forms and a short cry of fear. King Charlie looked up and saw that Skinny had bounded from the ground and now stood cowering near the windbreak with the light of the dying fire adrip from the long blade of his knife. Others of the tramps were also rising to form a bulwark for Skinny against the intruder.

The newcomer stood in the middle of the clearing with the wind flapping up the brim of his sombrero. He was a young fellow under twenty, with strongly made shoulders and a body not overtall, tapering rapidly toward the ground.

He stood now with his feet braced well apart, his bearing that of one ready to enter into any sort of action. His bearing was a cow-puncher's, the bandanna fluttering behind his neck, and the cartridge belt sagging about his hip by the weight of the heavy Colt which it supported.

But what was most of all noticeable was the glittering of the wild blue eyes. He looked wild cat and bulldog combined. It was no wonder that the hobos shrank away from him, and that, although they drew back toward Skinny as though ready to defend him, there was an uncertainty in the attitude of each man that promised the whole band would scatter if the youngster charged them.

For this very act he was teetering forward upon his toes when King Charlie, with a harsh cry of joy and strange sorrow combined, sprang to his feet, darted through the ranks of the tramps, and confronted The Kid.

"Billy!" he cried. "Billy English!"

The fire died from the eyes of the boy.

"Good Lord!" he gasped out. "How come you here? You!"

"I'm hunting for you. I couldn't stay away any longer, lad. And here I've found you just when I thought that the hunt was starting!"

He drew close. As though by mutual agreement, the two fell back so that their cautiously lowered voices were out of earshot of the staring, gaping tramps.

"I've got something to do here," Billy said. "Wait over yonder a minute, and I'll come back."

He slipped past King Charlie as he spoke, and started toward the hobos; but the old tramp caught him suddenly by the arm.

"I've got to do it," said Billy English. "I've been promising it to myself for a month!"

"You've got to do nothing of the kind," said King Charlie softly. "They're all laying for you, Billy. They'll shoot you to pieces if you start anything. Wait till you get him alone! Wait till you have a chance!"

Billy English writhed with distress, but the solid front which the tramps now presented to him was a convincing argument, and at length he turned with a sigh toward King Charlie.

"Sooner or later I got to get him," he said.

"All right," said King Charlie. "And I'll tell you this right now, son: This old world ain't so big but that you meet everybody twice that you meet once. You can tie to that idea, because it never fails. Come on, Billy."

Obediently Billy followed until they stood among the trees on the far side of the clearing, with the wind whistling shrilly about them, for

94

it was the middle of winter.

"We'll get out of here," said King Charlie. "It ain't healthful for you, son, even with me to look out for you now. Best thing we can do is to shift along. They tell me that you're doing most of your traveling on horses. Are you coming that way tonight?"

"I am," said Billy English. "But you can ride the hoss, dad. I'll walk. We can slide over to Cornwall City inside of an hour. Will that do you?"

"Fine," answered the "father," "except that I'll do the walking."

And on this he insisted when they reached Billy's horse on the lee of a sand hill. Despite all that Billy could say, King Charlie refused the saddle and strode away across the desert at his swinging stride, taking the smooth-going heel and toe at a rate that started Billy gasping in amazement.

CHAPTER XIII

BRUTALIZED

Prison and a year's life in yeggdom had certainly made a great difference. In a year of actual time, Billy English had added five years of apparent age. He had been a frolicsome boy at fifteen, only a man in his strength of arm and his trained agility and courage. At sixteen he was a man in his cold suspicions, his enormous hatreds, his contempt for everything and everybody, including himself. And all of these things could be traced back to the influence of King Charlie's lies which had set Billy adrift from his home village and an honest life.

The tramp shrugged such thoughts away for the time being and looked about him. There had been a rift in the massed, dull gray of the clouds which sheeted the sky. For a few seconds the moon looked through, her visage blurred continually by whirling mists.

That light was sufficient to show, however, the country through which they were traveling. The moment they left the tree-shaded hollow by the flag station, they had stepped onto a barren plain over which the wind swept in full career. This plain presently broke into naked hills. It was unfenced range.

Before them drifted a number of odd-shaped silhouettes; cattle were moving restlessly, helplessly down-wind. If the wind kept up and the snow continued to give an edge to its blasts, those cows might continue to move until they huddled under the hills which, in the distance, were a smudge beneath the sky line.

They finally arrived in view of a rambling little town tossed down without plan or reason among the hills. This was Cornwall City, though there was nothing about it to justify the second word of its title. The railroad did not tap it. It was a relic of the older days, when men built without reference to the possible direction which the iron rails might take through a vicinity.

Now it would never grow to a greater size. It lived on such mining and cattle and timber industries as flourished in the surrounding highlands, and continued its bleak existence in monotony broken at not infrequent intervals by the incursions of joyous cowboys bent on a good time.

Down to Cornwall City they came, with the town suddenly blotted out by the coming of snow. For the wind died, allowed an immensely thick curtain of flakes to commence falling, and then leaped up again from the horizon and hurled that mass of snow into the faces of the blinded travelers.

With numb hands and chattering teeth, The King looked on while Billy English led through the main street and around a big building to a barn behind, where he stabled the horse. He lighted a lantern which hung from a peg near the door, and by that light, as he passed down in the rear of the stalls, King Charlie caught glimpses of the finest group of horses he had ever seen. There was an instant differentiation between these, for instance, and the little cow pony from which Billy English had just dismounted; and the old tramp could not help noting it aloud.

"Look's to me," he said, "like some of the boys who lived at this hotel traveled in style, eh? Who owns these horses?"

"Which ones?" asked Billy, returning from giving his pony a feed of grain and hay.

"The gray and the chestnut beside him."

"Mine," said Billy.

"Both of 'em?"

He stepped nearer. No, they were not shams, but long-legged, narrow creatures meant for speed. There was much good material in them, to be sure.

"Your horses?" echoed the amazed King as he stepped back.

Billy English looked at him quietly, and at length shrugged his shoulders as though he did not care to reveal the whole truth even to one with whom a confidence could be placed in entire safety.

"I have to travel long stages sometimes," he said. "That's why I need 'em."

"And the other horses?" asked The King. "What about that big black?"

"That belongs to Hoyt. When you see him, you'll understand why the black has to be big.

Joe weighs a ton, pretty near, and he needs a hoss made the same way."

"And the brown horse at the end?"

"Belongs to Dean. Now d'you know enough?"

"And the three of you all work —"

"Shut up!" snarled Billy English.

He stepped up to his "father" with the quick, gliding step of a pugilist, and his face was an ugly one to watch.

"You mind your tongue when you're around with me," said Billy English. "Ask all the questions you want to, but don't ask 'em loud. Understand?"

"Anything you say," answered The King calmly, but in his heart he wondered. This young savage was certainly not the boy he had first drawn astray the year before. In twelve months he had been thoroughly brutalized.

"Now come on with me," said Billy English.

He led the way to the rear door of the house, and there he paused again and waited in the snow-storm while he delivered himself of another ultimatum.

"Look here," he said. "When you get inside the hotel, you may have a lot of folks asking you questions. Well, you don't know nothing; you see?"

"I see."

"Don't forget it! I'm going to take care of you if I can. But I ain't going to be bothered more'n I have to. You let me grow up any way that looked good to me, and now when you come around you can use me for a meal ticket, but you can't use me no other way. Have you got that straight?"

King Charlie, no matter what anger he may have felt, simply nodded.

CHAPTER XIV

A SMALL VOICE

IT was never intended for use in such a climate as that of Cornwall City. Those thin pine boards had been warped loose by the fires of summer, and then soaked and rotted and wrenched at by the snows and winds of winter, until now every gust was split into myriad small voices which ran whispering through the building. The clothes of King Charlie were plucked at softly by the drafts as he climbed up the groaning stairs behind Billy English, lighted on the way by the flame which fluttered in the throat of a smoky chimney from where the lamp was placed at the landing.

In the upper hall, having passed one of two doors, Billy English struck the next heavily with his fist by way of announcement that he was about to enter, and then turned the knob and kicked the door open.

The scene within revealed animal comfort to such a degree that King Charlie, drawing the door to behind him, was amazed. A fairly thick rug lay upon the floor. Heavy curtains on the inside of the door and the window minimized the drafts which worked in around these major openings. Upon the table stood two bottles of bootleg whisky, with glasses handy.

A stove glowed red hot in a corner of the room, with a pan of water simmering on the top in case any one should desire to make, with hot water and sugar and lemons, which were spread in quantity on the little kitchen table adjoining, a hot punch. Moreover, there was a coffeepot on a corner of the table, and a can of coffee beside it. Not that the room gave the appearance of a housekeeping apartment. It was simply equipped with such conveniences as would be most appreciated on a cold winter's day. The two cots at the sides of the room were made up with plenty of soft, thick blankets, and there was an extra supply of cushions in case the lodgers desired to lounge there.

As for the other appointments of the room, they were chiefly guns of all varieties in racks and hanging in holsters along the wall along with all manner of clothes, most of them muddy. An open door hinted that there was another room to the suite which Billy English and his associates occupied.

These associates, in the meantime, were sitting at the main table in the exact center of the room engaged in a friendly little game of poker. The hungry eyes of King Charlie fixed instantly on the heaps of greenbacks which were the stakes, and even as he entered he heard a low voice say: "Bet fifty!"

What manner of men were these who could afford to bet fifty dollars at a throw?

It needed only a glance to tell him. Yonder tall,

long-faced, sad-eyed fellow with the pathetic and many-wrinkled smile — that was The Dean, an expert "dauber" and otherwise a gambler of parts, who was also possessed of a variety of talents so that he could turn his attention to almost anything and acquit himself well. It amazed King Charlie to see such a celebrity in such company, for Billy English was only a child, comparatively speaking.

The second player was a sharp contrast with the tall man. This unquestionably must be Joe Hoyt of whom Billy had said that he weighed a ton. His great shoulders pressed back so that the top of the chair was almost buried in the overhang of relaxed muscles. His big head was set, apparently, without the use of a neck, squarely in the middle of the vast shoulders. Below the shoulders he did not taper to the waistline. He was straight up and down from the armpits to the floor, where his bulk was distributed upon two large, shapeless feet.

This man now rose and whirled to his feet, because his back was to the door; The King found himself looking into a thick-featured but rather handsome face, which at once smiled cordial greeting on Billy and turned to The King himself with a frank scowl of question.

Billy English sailed his hat across the room and flung himself down on a couch.

"Hoyt," he growled out, "and Dean, meet my father. This is King Charlie. I think I've heard you talk about him, Dean."

The Dean nodded gravely to King Charlie.

103

"How are you?" he inquired politely as he shook hands. "Of course I remember you, King. But I never was wised up about you being a family man. Shake hands with Joe Hoyt. Hoyt, this is King Charlie. Maybe you've never bumped into him, because he don't often come out as far West as you do. But Charlie is the king of them all."

"Yes?" drawled Hoyt, unconvinced.

"The chief reason," said The Dean, "is because he never looks any older!"

In the meantime, Billy English had rolled from the couch to his feet and sauntered into the next room. Instantly the expression on the face of The Dean was changed.

"Look here!" he whispered to The King. "What's the play? The kid is ours. Where do you expect to horn in, Charlie?"

"My own kin," said King Charlie. "You can't expect a man to give up that, can you?"

"Kin — Charlie, do I look that much of a simp? There ain't a sign of you in him!"

"No, he's his mother's son; there's no doubt of that," and the old rascal sighed.

"You're going to try to make your play with him, eh?" asked The Dean darkly.

"It ain't anything that you boys can stop," cautioned The King, speaking as guardedly as they in his reply. "Now watch out. He's coming back. Only lay to this: I ain't trying to spoil anything you birds have planned."

So saying, he raised his voice to a hearty greeting for Hoyt just as Billy English returned. He crossed the room to the table, poured out a drink of whisky, and shoved it toward King Charlie. But King Charlie refused it, and Billy English tossed off the drink at a swallow and began to pace up and down the room. The Dean and Joe Hoyt paused to look anxiously after him, and then they forced themselves to continue their game; but it could easily be seen that their interest was entirely perfunctory.

The boy, turning again on Charlie, seemed to remember something; he hastily shoved a chair near the stove and pointed to it.

"Sit down," he commanded, "and get warmed up."

"I'd rather get thawed out gradual," said King Charlie. "Don't worry about me. I'll take care of myself, son."

"Lay off that 'son' talk, too," barked Billy English. "Maybe I am, but nothing is bought by telling the world about it."

He stopped at the table in his hurried pacing and swigged off another big portion of the whisky.

"You're hitting it up pretty hard, kid," said The Dean. "You better watch that stuff."

"Never mind me," said Billy English. "I'll handle my own liquor without no little helping words from you gents. Now, what's planted?"

The other two started and flashed glances at King Charlie. These glances plainly said: "You fool! Do you expect us to talk before a stranger?"

"I told you he was my father," said Billy. "Anything you can say to me you can say to him. I ask you ag'in: What you got planted?"

Hoyt, whose back was turned to Billy, winked at The Dean as one who had no solution for the problem himself, and bade The Dean talk or remain silent as he felt best. The Dean decided on silence.

"Haven't anything certain," he said. "Nothing worth talking about. Besides, what's the good? Can't ride on a night like this."

"Can't ride on a night like this?" cried Billy English, sneering. "Why not? Because they's a little snow in the air, will that hurt you? And ain't Warnerville dead ahead down the wind? We could hit it before morning."

"Wait a minute!" exclaimed The Dean. "You ain't in earnest, Billy?"

"Why not? The snow and the cold and the wind, that make your gents think that we can't make the play in Warnerville, is just the reasons that the boys in Warnerville won't think that we'll come, if they got any suspicions about it. And so we drop in, clean up, and make a get-away in the falling snow — that covers up our tracks as fast as we make 'em! Ain't that easy?"

"Billy, what makes you so hot on this trail? Ain't you fixed easy enough? Why, you could lay off for a year on what you've made lately!"

"You're wrong," answered Billy. "I ain't got enough to pay for one gambling lesson from The Dean!"

Here he stepped a little forward and looked at The Dean so narrowly that the latter changed color.

"Billy," he hastened to protest, "you know as well as I do that I was only jollying you when I kept that money I won from you the other day. I don't want it. I told you right off that I didn't want it, and I say it again to-day. You can have it —"

"Bah!" sneered Billy. "I ain't a welsher, and you know I ain't! Shut up the windy talk, Dean. You can't work it with me. I'm tired of it!"

The Dean flushed, looked down, and hesitated. Plainly he would rather have teeth pulled than force this issue, but his self-respect forced him ahead.

"Billy," he said gently, "I can't let you talk to me like that. I've done nothing to deserve it, and I can't sit here and let you talk that way! Not if you was as old as this bird that calls himself your father!"

"You can't stand for it?" scoffed Billy. "You got to stand for it! Oh, I know the pair of you. I know how you're playing your dirty game. But I let it go! I know that I'm the door opener for you; I get you inside the safe, and then you and Hoyt pull down the loot, and you let me off with anything you think is enough to pay me for my trouble!"

Accumulated anger seemed to be boiling in him. He effervesced with rage.

"When we got away from Glenn Lake, who was it that pulled the posse down the wrong trail while you and Hoyt got off slick and easy, and you with a lame hoss, Dean? But out of that job, you held out on me. You held out a whole handful of big greenbucks that —"

"That's not true!" cried The Dean, white-faced with anger and nervousness as he saw the crisis approaching. "Billy, for Heaven's sake don't let that murdering temper of yours run away with you. Let me tell you the straight of it! What we got out of that —"

"Don't talk!" cried Billy.

And yet every word had been spoken softly, with all the accents of rage conveyed in voices often no louder than strong whispers. "Don't talk!" he commanded again. "It — it makes me want to tear your hearts out! I know the coin that you've been sending away. And what have I got left? A measly thousand! A rotten thousand!"

"Because you throw your money away. Every bum that asks for a handout, you give half of what you've got. Is that —"

"That's different from what you gents do, ain't it? Yes, I'll tell a man that it's a lot different! You got not a cent to waste on the unlucky ones. But I been making up my mind that I've traveled the same trail with you boys far enough. It seems to me that you two fit in too pretty together to need me with you. I'm quitting!"

He scowled at them with such unreasoning and sullen rage that King Charlie gasped. The last speech had stirred both The Dean and huge Hoyt from speech to action. They came threateningly close to the boy.

"You aim to draw out on us?" they said hotly.

"After everything is set and planned for —"

They stopped, flashed a vicious glance at King Charlie, whose presence kept them from mentioning names, and roared in unison at Billy English, forgetting the thin walls of the house: "We'll see you dead before we let you pull out on us!"

Their near approach had driven Billy back until his shoulders were pressed against the wall, and from this point his bright blue eyes glittered at the two big men. He was not in the least afraid; but plainly he was in a fighting rage, and wanted merely to balance accounts before he attacked them. And though King Charlie trembled for what might happen, he was tongue-tied in admiration of the dauntless courage of the boy.

"If you see me dead," said Billy, "you'll both of you follow me! I'll take you both along, you thickheads! Start something, Dean! Go for your gat, Hoyt. I'm waiting!"

Their answer was an inarticulate growl of rage, and the three men hung trembling on the balance of fierce action. King Charlie, cold as a fish when a fight was imminent, saw that his previous quietness had taken him out of their attention, and that they were not guarding against him. Accordingly, he glided to the nearest gun rack and secured a revolver.

It had hardly touched his palm, however, when there was a loud rattle at the doorknob, the door was opened, and a sharp, small voice called: "I wish you please wouldn't make so much noise in here!"

Hoyt and The Dean glanced over their shoulders and saw in the open doorway a little five-year-old girl with a tumble of bright hair about a pale face, and they staggered back from Billy English as though he had suddenly pointed two guns at them.

CHAPTER XV

WHO WILL PROVIDE?

THE last to see her was Billy English; but when he did, the effect upon him was even more startling. He brushed out of his eyes the bristle of hair which had fallen across them, and he ground his knuckles across his forehead as though he would banish a dream which afflicted him.

"How come the kid here?" he gasped out. And he repeated: "Who brought her here?"

King Charlie, through the power of greater age, became the controlling factor in the room. He went to the little girl.

"Who are you?" he asked.

"Louise Alison Dora Young," said the child, rolling up her eyes with adorable gravity. "And my mother says you should ought to be quiet."

King Charlie, glad of the interruption which promised to prolong the life of his protégé, sat down on the nearest chair and lifted Louise Alison Dora Young to his knee. He uttered an exclamation of dismay as he did so.

"Darned if she ain't all skin and bones!" he cried at his companions.

The girl shook her head at him in serious disapproval.

"You shouldn't say 'ain't,' " she told him.

"I won't," said The King obediently. "I'll keep inside the fences you put up. But where's your mother, honey?"

"She's right over across the hall," said Louise. "She's sick, and she can't go to sleep when you make so much noise."

"Oh!" exclaimed Hoyt. "Your mother is here, eh?" And he exchanged significant glances with The Dean.

"I guess she is sick," said Hoyt. "Can we do anything for her?"

"No," answered Louise Alison Dora Young. "All she wants is to be left alone. She wants quiet. She just cries when there's noise!"

She conveyed that strange information with another shake of her head.

"Look at her neck," said King Charlie, grown suddenly husky with horror and rage. "She ain't had enough to eat, this baby. D'you live in the same house with —"

He checked himself out of respect for the big, questioning eyes which flashed up to him. But, still staring at the others, he pointed out the starved, small throat of Louise. The three men gathered about in a stunned and stupid semicircle and gaped at her.

"What'll we do?" they asked The King. She became a little frightened under this steady scrutiny, and swept their faces in dismay until her eyes rested on the younger and more handsome face of Billy English. Then a smile wavered into life on her pale lips. Suddenly she put out her arms toward him, and Billy English gasped.

"What'll I do?" he asked of The King.

The King laughed heartily. "That means she's looked the rest of us over," he declared, "and decided that you're the one that she picks out. Take her up in your arms. That's what she wants. She's tired of me!"

Billy English flushed to the eyes with pleasure, and then he awkwardly obeyed. He raised her in his strong young arms, and suddenly tossed her up and caught her as she came down, a maneuver that brought a peal of laughter from Louise. The laugh was echoed by three deep, pleased chuckles from the onlookers.

But Billy English had grown dark of brow again.

"You're right, King," he said; "she's all skin and bones. And —"

He broke off short, turned, and went hastily to the table; there, from a covered little tin can, he took out a piece of bread. It had been cut the evening before, and the close proximity of the stove's heat had warped and withered it. This he raised, but no sooner was it in sight than Louise Young uttered a shrill cry and tore it from his hands. The next instant she was tearing it to pieces with an animal greed.

Hoyt and The Dean bowed their heads in mute shame and horror, and King Charlie watched agape. As for Billy English, he had turned livid with conflicting emotions.

"And her mother?" asked Billy suddenly. "Maybe that's why she —"

"Don't talk that way!" cried The Dean, answering before the accusation was completed. "You talk like a fool, Billy. But —"

"We're going to go see," said Billy. "And if it's happened the way I think it's happened, we'll all of us burn through eternity, boys!"

He led the way through the door with the others behind him. On the way, King Charlie hastily made his inquiries. He learned from Joe Hoyt that they had several times, during the past three or four days, noticed a woman who lodged across the hall from them, and who seemed excessively thin and wan and languid, moving slowly, with dark-shadowed eyes cast always down.

In the meantime, they had reached the door of the bedroom across the way, and here Billy English lowered the child to the floor, where she at once opened the door and stepped on tiptoe inside, turning her head to warn them, with her finger pressed to her lips, that they must preserve silence.

She disappeared and came back after a moment to say: "She's sound asleep! She's tried a long, long time to go to sleep and couldn't."

"Why not?" whispered Billy English, and the others leaned closer to hear the answer.

"Because something hurts her inside," said Louise.

"Starvation," said King Charlie slowly. "That's it. If a woman'll let her baby get as thin as this kid is, you can bet that she is a wreck herself.

114

How long has it been since your mother ate anything, Louise?"

"She doesn't eat any more," said Louise. "She stopped days and days ago, because she says that it makes her sick to eat. Isn't that a queer way to be?"

"And us throwing away coin drinking and — You go into the room again," said Hoyt, "and wake up your mother and tell her that you got a friend out in the hall that wants to see her. Will you do that?"

"She nodded, slipped through the door, and presently they could hear her calling, first softly and then more loudly. And all at once, with a sort of stifled scream, she ran back to the door and sprang among them, huddling close to Billy English.

"I'm afraid!" she cried. "I'm afraid! Oh, why won't she talk to me!"

The four strong men were turned to stone. At length the tramp stepped slowly to the door and paused there to look back, in case any of the others might have the courage to accompany him. But they merely gaped at him with frozen dismay.

So he faced the interior of the room again, dragged off his hat, and with a slow and uncertain step, he disappeared.

They heard his footsteps cease. They waited in mortal silence, and then they heard a hurrying footfall come back toward the door.

King Charlie came shuddering back and looked

at them. One glance was enough.

"Your mother wants to sleep, honey," he managed to say to Louise. "We'll take you in and keep you warm by the fire for a while."

He took her hand, but his own was shaking so much that she withdrew her fingers, and Billy English had to pick her up again. In the rooms of the three long riders they deposited her.

King Charlie gave orders. "Billy," he said, "you stay here and keep Louise happy. Dean, come with me. I'll have to use you, Hoyt, too."

They followed him reluctantly into the hall. There, in hushed voices, they conferred.

"We never guessed," protested big Hoyt to the old tramp, as though King Charlie were judge and jury with power of giving and taking life. "How could we have ever guessed that she was really down and out and —"

"Never mind telling me about it," said King Charlie coldly. "I ain't the one to blame you. It's everybody else in the world that'll do the talking when they hear about gents that let a woman starve to death in the same house that they're drinking in. But you go down and tell the landlady — or whoever runs this place. Hoyt, you go down and tell her. Dean, you come in with me."

The Dean stalked slowly behind him while big Hoyt shambled off down the hall.

In the meantime, they entered the death chamber, and there The Dean saw a still form on the bed. He, like the tramp, dragged the hat automatically from his head as he approached. A single glance at her face was sufficient to suggest in what manner she had passed away. The eyes were still open and gazing wearily at eternity. The Dean closed them.

After that he was able to speak.

"What are we going to do next?" he asked.

"Maybe this lady will know," answered King Charlie.

As he spoke, steps came hurriedly up the hall and approached the room, and they could hear a woman's sharp voice chattering busily to Joe Hoyt while the yegg ventured only mumbled replies. At the door of the room King Charlie saw a virago appear. She planted her fists upon her hips and glowered at the form on the bed.

"I might of knowed!" she moaned. "I might of knowed what was going to happen when she put off paying me — but I always let my soft heart make a fool out of me! I always do!"

"Maybe you do," said The King, "but the important thing now is: Where are her friends?"

"If I knew that, d'you think I'd be worrying?"

"Where did she come from?"

"From the camp down the road. She's been cooking for the logging camp. She's been there since fall."

"Well?"

"Well, she got fired, that's all. She come to town and got sick and spent all her money — and there she is now left on my hands when —"

"Wait a minute," said King Charlie. "You ain't going to be made to pay for nothing. We'll tend to all that. Only thing you can contribute is a little free information."

She was immensely relieved by the prospect.

"You don't know nothing about where she come from or who her folks might be?"

"Nothing except that she calls herself Mrs. Young."

"That's rock bottom all you know?"

"Yes."

"Then we're going to go through her things in that trunk over yonder. Know where the key is?"

"In the top bureau drawer."

They found it, and unlocked the big trunk which stood close to the window on the far side of the room; but when the heavy top was lifted, they stared down into stark emptiness. There was not even a rag within!

Here the landlady cried: "See what's happened? She's burned everything! Look around the stove!"

They could see on the floor around the stove a handful of bits of papers, odd corners and margins which had blown out, perhaps, when the door of the stove was opened to shove more in. She had felt that death was near her, and she had destroyed the clews to her back trail before she left the earth.

"And the brat?" cried the landlady. "Who's going to take care of her?"

CHAPTER XVI

A PROTECTIVE ALLIANCE

Here The Dean wrinkled his long face in disapproving anger. "Don't call her a brat," he said sternly. "The care of her ain't going to fall on you, ma'am, and you can start betting on that right now."

A bitter life had made her what she was, hardened to perfect distrust of all things and particularly of all persons. But the scorn and the anger in the voice of The Dean, and the sick disgust in the face of Hoyt and King Charlie, wakened shame in her.

"And who else is there to take in the poor, forlorn kiddy?" she asked in a whining voice.

"I'll take her!" cried King Charlie magnificently. "I'll take her and give her a home!"

As he spoke, a picture of his own "home" darted in a thousand images across his mind's eye. He saw the inside of an "empty," noisy as a madhouse, bumping along at fifty an hour. He saw a stray corner in a cellar. He saw an open fire in the jungle. No wonder that King Charlie blinked as he thought of these things; and yet he maintained a dauntless front to the others. His statement had roused them to admiration of such reckless self-sacrifice. Not

119

one of them had had a true dependent, and they were amazed by The King.

"As for this poor woman," said The King, stepping to the bed, "I dunno but she's a millionaire's wife that's run off because of trouble to home. Nobody can tell. Leastwise, none of us can tell!"

"That's true," said big Hoyt. "She had the look of a high stepper even when she was —"

He choked over the word "starving" and became silent, staring gloomily at the floor.

"All right, Hoyt," said King Charlie. "Suppose you go out and make arrangements to take care of the body."

Hoyt nodded and hurried out to find the undertaker. Meantime, the landlady, feeling that she was no longer needed, slipped away without a sound, and King Charlie and The Dean went toward the room where they had left Billy English and the little girl.

"Pardner," said The Dean slowly, halting his companion in the hall, "do you mind telling me what you figure on gaining by putting up the bluff about being the father of Billy English?"

"Bluff?" said the tramp. "That ain't a bluff, son. Not a bit of a bluff. That's the painful fact!"

The Dean growled. "I ain't aiming to start no sort of trouble with you at a time like this," he said; "but I got to say that Hoyt and me ain't fools. We know your game. You've sicked him onto us with a lot of talk about how much money he could make with you, and how little he's making with us! But we ain't going to let you get away with it. Don't forget!" He added with a growing fury: "Otherwise, what should have sent him home ready to eat raw meat like this?"

"Dean," said the tramp, "it means nothing to me, that sort of game. I'm not trying to get him to go away with me. If you doubt it, wait and see. He came here raving, partly because you gents have been using him pretty cheap, mostly because he went out on a trail to-night, and, instead of getting his man, he ran into a dozen hobos all ready to fight at once. So he came away without licking his man. That's what put him off his feed."

"Was that why he went out?" murmured The Dean. He shook his head. "We saw him go out late this afternoon, but we didn't have no idea where he was bound. Guess he must have got some tip that his man was pretty close. That's the straight of it, eh? He's just crazy with disappointment, not up to any deviltry that you've put into him?"

"Not a bit," The King assured him. "Listen now to that!"

From the room they could hear, in a lull of the wind, the voice of Billy English, softened, and singing one of those eerie melodies with which the cowpunchers, riding night herd, lull the cattle.

"She's plumb knocked him off his feet," said The Dean, grinning broadly, as though that song had put him out of all thought of the hostile intentions which he had just been cherishing against the tramp.

So saying, he jerked the door open and exposed

121

Billy English seated near the stove, with Louise Young cradled in his arms, and singing blissfully to her sleepy ears and to the ceiling. He stopped his song and flushed a little, scowling at the intruders. Then he managed to raise one finger to warn them into silence. The child slept.

They tiptoed awkwardly in, and Billy English carried the girl into the next room and deposited her on the couch there. He returned, closed the door, and announced in triumph that he had been able to put her down and cover her without wakening her.

"It's the bread and the warmth of the stove," said King Charlie. "She's apt to sleep quite a little while, and when she wakes up we'll have the other thing finished, I hope."

He indicated his meaning still further by a gesture over his shoulder, and the others went slowly to their chairs and sat down.

"After all," said The Dean at length, "it ain't our fault, is it? Ain't there other people in the house besides us?"

"She was right across the hall from us," said Billy English, "and we was in here drinking and wasting more'n enough chuck to have kept her and the baby. How old might she be, King?"

"About five. She's got name enough for fifty. What is it? Louise Alison Dora Young? Take her quite a spell to write even her initials."

The others were thoughtful for a second, and then Billy exclaimed: "D'you know what those initials make?"

"Well?" they queried.

" 'Lady' is what they spell, L-a-d-y, as plain as day! And maybe that's what her mother was — and what she's going to be — a lady! Notice how she talks? Just like a little book, by —"

"You can't be talking like that around her," said The King.

"There won't be much chance to talk around her," said Billy. "Soon as she wakes up, I suppose she'll be gone some place to find her relatives."

"She ain't got none," The King assured him.

They told him briefly how they had examined the room and found nothing in it which could serve as a clew to the identity of the dead woman and her child. The Dean even concluded the account with King Charlie's avowal that he would take care of the little girl, and the landlady's willingness to hand over the child to him. To all of this Billy English listened with the greatest interest until the end, when he turned on King Charlie with a growl, his ugly, quick temper changing his face.

"And what right in the name of Heaven," he cried, "have you got to say that you'll take care of a kid like her — a lady like she's going to be — when you can't even take care of yourself?"

"If a gent has the heart, he'll find the way," declared The King, undaunted. "Besides, Billy, you got to find a better way than that to talk to your own father."

"Show me a reason," snapped Billy, "why I should talk soft to you?"

"So's you'll keep from spoiling the manners of

the kid," said King Charlie with great calm.

"Damn the kid and the rest of you!" answered Billy with a black look, and in such a loud voice that there was a faint cry from the next room.

Billy English, with a gasp, glided to the door of the room, opened it softly, and disappeared within. A moment later they could hear him talking softly to soothe the child.

The Dean swore in muffled astonishment as soon as the door had closed.

"Who'd ever think of a young bulldog like him being so careful with a baby?" he demanded. "Who'd ever think of it? He's been like a starved wolf ever since we've knowed him, so far as temper goes!"

"It's his mother working out in him," replied King Charlie. "Me, I'm a rough one. I don't try to hide that. But his mother was fine as silk. And look how it sticks out in Billy! Birds of a feather — you know. That's what makes him and the girl so thick. She picked him out of the lot of us and held up her arms to him, and he sticks around her as if he was her real father. You can't explain things like that away!"

"I won't try to," answered The Dean slowly, and, going to the table, he picked up the pack of cards and began to shuffle, slipping the halves of the pack into each other with such oiled dexterity that King Charlie's eye glistened with approval. He could tell the master gambler at a glance.

But his skill with the cards did not appease the

gloom which was rising in The Dean, and presently he tossed the pack from him, rose, and took from beneath one of the beds a case out of which he drew a violin. He tuned it hastily, tucked it at length into place under his chin, and, tilting far back in his chair until his shoulders touched the wall and his head was cramped forward, he closed his eyes and drew out sweet and melancholy strains. So light was his muted touch that each note was no louder than a whisper; but so deft was the bowing that every note was, in that thin compass, rounded and true.

Of such matters The King was no good critic, but he knew enough to admire again, and he began to set The Dean down as no common man. For his own part, a scheme which promised him at least some days of peace and rest was growing in his mind.

So he sat back and said not a word until big Hoyt came into the room, shook the snow from his shoulders, and with a glance at each of them announced more plainly than words that the business was completed and the body removed from the house. Here Billy English returned to the room, shutting the door behind him deftly and noiselessly.

"She's sleeping again," he announced to them in a triumphant whisper.

He crossed to the stove and warmed his hands at it. Then he turned, still smiling.

"She's a lady, right enough," he declared. "All I did was to tell her everything was all right, and she needn't worry about nothing. She wanted her mother at first, but pretty soon she tucked her hand inside of mine, give me a smile, and went off sound to sleep."

He chuckled contentedly at the thought, and King Charlie decided that this was the most opportune possible moment to make his proposal. He rose and thereby drew their attention.

"Boys," he said, "it looks to me that the only end that Lady is coming to is an orphan asylum pretty soon."

This announcement was greeted with a groan.

"There's only one way to stop it," said King Charlie.

They wanted to know, in one voice, what it might be.

"She might be adopted," said King Charlie.

"Who by?"

"By us," said The King.

They gaped at him.

"I mean it," he went on, developing his thought. "If one man can adopt a son or a daughter, why couldn't the four of us shake hands all around and agree that we'd adopt her? Why not?"

They blinked at the suggestion.

"You're out of your head," said The Dean at last. "What's the average life of a — of them that live the way we do? How long would she have any adopted fathers?"

"That's the beauty of it," said King Charlie. "Any one of us ain't apt to last long, but out of the four of us, one is pretty sure to keep going.

Besides, boys, if we should take Lady with us, we'd have something that would tie us all together and make us strong. What was it that smoothed out all the wrinkles a while back when Billy and you two was having words? Well, it was Lady coming to the door of the room and giving us a call. That means something, pals. That was more'n an accident. If we had her to work for, we'd all stick and work for one another. Ain't that logic?"

"You mean," corrected Joe Hoyt sarcastically, "that we'd do the working, and that you'd stay around at home with Lady?"

But here Billy English interrupted: "Gents, if we could try that, you'd sure see me working all day every day and never asking no questions!"

The Dean had been about to shake his head, but now he paused to consider, and at length he became serious and his eye brightened. Many and many a thousand dollars could be made by association with Billy English if the lad were manageable, and the presence of Louise Alison Dora Young promised to make him entirely amenable to reason.

"Well, boys," said The Dean, "I think King Charlie has an idea. If you and me, Hoyt, stay to business; and if Billy English stops running off every now and then to hunt down some bo that's bothered him — if them things was to happen, we could afford to have King Charlie staked out somewhere keeping a home for us, and Lady could be in that home. King, is that your idea?"

127

"You take the words right out of my mouth, Dean!"

"Shake on it!" cried Billy English, and in his enthusiasm he ran about the room wringing their hands one after the other.

"You might say," said Joe Hoyt, who seemed the least joyous of the lot, "that we're a bunch of fools organizing a company for the sake of a kid we ain't knowed for more'n a couple of hours. But — it's something new, boys, anyway!"

CHAPTER XVII

TWELVE THOUSAND APIECE

WHAT," asked King Charlie, "are we to do about telling Lady —"

"You do no telling," said Billy English. "I've fixed that already. Her mother went on a little trip, and'll be back for Lady later on. I've told her all that, and she's happy."

This fragment of conversation occurred later in the evening before a late supper, and when they descended to the dining room, Louise Young, so newly named "Lady," was carried on the broad shoulders of Hoyt, while a trail of silver-thin laughter floated up the stairs behind her.

Many a time during that meal the four grew gloomy when they watched the smiling face and heard the piping voice of the little girl and thought, in contrast, of the dead mother. But they agreed that it was better thus. On the next day the body would be buried, and Lady should know nothing of what had happened. Far better that she should never connect her mother with the thought of death.

Afterward there was a gay party in the rooms upstairs. The Dean played his gayest tunes on his fiddle to the immense delight of Lady, and when she was bundled off to bed they sat down to another consultation as to her future. Funds were in the first place put into the hands of The King to buy her clothes in such quantities as might be advised by some woman of the village. After that they argued long and earnestly as to the best location for their permanent headquarters where King Charlie was to establish their home while the three struck out here and there through the country and brought back what plunder they might gather. Of course there was one great added danger in any such plan. Even in this town they felt that they had stayed too long for safety. But, if they settled down permanently with Lady and King Charlie, their home might sooner or later prove a trap in which the law could bag them all.

In the midst of this discussion there was a knock at the door, which was immediately opened by Hoyt to expose a youth with one of those faces which can only be described as crime-battered. He was in his early twenties, handsome, smiling; but half a dozen scars seamed his features. His eyes, in moments of relaxation, were dull; and his walk was somewhat halting.

They greeted him with acclaim. Every one saving Billy English knew him of old, and Billy himself was quickly made acquainted.

"Here's Billy English, Jack. Here's Jack Turner, Billy. You boys must have heard of each other. He started a shade later than you, Jack. But he's sure used his first year in great shape when it comes to making a name for himself!"

They shook hands, at the same time estimating each other's force with sharp glances.

"Yep," said Jack, "I've heard a good deal about you, Billy. Matter of fact, that's one of the big reasons that I've dropped in on you boys. There's something ahead that needs doing, and I figure you fellows have the layout to suit me! Can I use you?"

"If we can use you," said The Dean, "we got nothing against being used."

"Well," said Jack Turner, "you know me. I ain't the kind that tries to grab everything for himself. You can trust me, I guess."

They agreed, in chorus, that they could.

"But you, Charlie," said Turner to the veteran tramp, "don't have to listen in on this."

"Don't you trust me?" asked King Charlie, somewhat offended.

"I trust nobody," said Jack Turner. "I don't aim that at you, Charlie. Everybody knows that you're as straight as they come. But I ain't throwing no talk that'll be useful to you, so why should you sidetrack near a temptation?"

King Charlie waved his hand in agreement and left the room for that in which Lady slept, only to drop on his knees and press his ear against the keyhole to such effect that he was able to hear enough fragments of the talk to get its general purport.

He heard Jack Turner quickly outline his plan to the others. He knew of a large shipment of money which was heading west, and he had determined to stop the train and blow the safe for the money. He himself was an expert all around, but he would be glad to have such a professional as Joe Hoyt to lend a hand. The Dean would be welcome in many details, such as holding back the train crew and keeping the passengers herded inside the train. As for the stopping of the train, that would be best undertaken by some one who had never before been connected with a robbery of that character, for he understood that the train would be literally loaded down with guards.

No doubt one of these guards would be riding the blind baggage, as the train struck the mountains, to make sure that no one swung up onto that platform, from which it was a simple matter for an armed man to climb over the tender and down into the cab and hold up the engineer and fireman. But this was exactly what must be dared and what must be accomplished in order to stop the train.

If there were two guards riding the blind baggage, as the closed end of the first baggage car is termed, it simply meant that the man who attempted to climb on there would be either kicked off to his death as a mere hobo, or else captured and held as a more dangerous possibility.

And if only one guard were riding the blind baggage, it was barely possible that an expert, fearless and quick of movement, might be able to climb onto the platform in spite of him. At least the odds would give him one chance in ten!

Further, if there were no guard at all, the only hazard to begin with would be the dangers of leaping for the handrail when the train was in rapid motion.

In short, this was a task for which the crippled Turner would have immediately chosen himself in the old days; but now, unfortunately, he was far too stiff and slow for such work. The Dean and Joe Hoyt were possibilities, to be sure; but best of all would be one who united practiced agility and the nimble feet of youth with perfect courage and uncommon coolness and strength.

This man, to be plain, was Billy English. To get him, Jack Turner had traveled several hundred miles by train and by horseback. For the sake of swinging Billy into the deal, it seemed that Jack had given the cold shoulder to a dozen old pals, men who had ridden the length and the breadth of the mountain desert with him on one sort of errand or another.

"Because, kid," said Jack Turner, leaning over and talking out of the side of his mouth, after the fashion of men who have learned the ways of the prisons through bitter years of experience, "I've tried 'em all out, and, though I know a bunch that are good, I've got to get one now that's a dead sure thing!"

But Billy English shook his head and rose.

"I ought to have told you sooner," he said, "but it's just been growing up in my mind while I heard you talking, pardner. In that other room — which you can't be expected to know things that you ain't seen — there's a little girl that I've got to look after. No matter what I might be wanting to do, the thing that I have to do is to look after Lady. Well, Jack, I'm going to do that by getting a steady job and working as a puncher on some layout."

The news dazed the others.

At length The Dean cried: "Good Lord, Billy, what d'you mean? D'you know what a puncher's wages are?"

"I know that they're mighty small," said Billy, "but they're mighty sure."

Joe Hoyt started to his feet. "Billy," he began, "if you —"

"Shut up, boys," said Jack Turner. "I got something more to say that'll sound good to him. Listen!"

He leaned over and tapped the words into the palm of one hand with the stiff fingers of the other.

"In that safe on that train, d'you think there's some small-time bunch of lunch money, Billy? D'you think that I've come all this way to get next to you with any little stake hanging in the air? Listen to me, son: There's going to be seventy-five thousand dollars soaked away in that safe. Seventy-five thousand — understand? And it's going to be ours. You're going to start to-night and ride like blazes till you get to Williamstown, and then you're going to wait there till to-morrow night. And to-morrow night you're going to grab the blind baggage when she comes through on the express. You're going to climb onto the tender and drop down into the cab when the engine begins to snake along into Jeffrey Pass. Understand?"

Billy shook his head. "It sounds good," he said, "and I'd like to work it with you. But not for me, Jack!"

"Lost your nerve?"

"Don't say that," said Billy. "You get me nervous when you begin to talk that way to me, Jack! I'm staying behind for the little girl. That's why!"

"Then you're a fool. How many of us are there? Four. Four ain't many to hold up a train, but every man here is the right stuff, and I'd rather have four good ones than forty common bos. But four into seventy-five makes something pretty fat. One third goes out to them that tipped the shipment to me. That leaves fifty. Divide that by four. Leaves you twelve thousand five hundred apiece. After you've got that wadded down in your jeans you can afford to resign. Take this chance, and afterward you and the kid are on Easy Street. Does that sound to you, Billy? Twelve thousand five hundred! Out of that you can fix her up. You can send her away to school. You can raise her like a lady!"

At the last word Billy English started and groaned.

"She is a lady," he said. "And how could I raise her the way she ought to be raised unless I got the coin?"

He turned sharply upon Jack Turner.

"I'm with you!" he said. "Tell me the rest!"

135

CHAPTER XVIII

THE TREASURE TRAIN

It was cold midnight when Billy saddled, not the cow pony on which The King had seen him mounted earlier in the evening, but one of those tall, leggy horses which King Charlie had wondered about. At the same time, the other three were making their own mounts ready and agreeing with King Charlie on the rendezvous.

No sooner were they under way than he was to gather their effects in their rooms and make ready for a departure early the next morning, rain or hail or snow. They directed him toward the spot in the mountains at which he should aim with the buckboard and horses belonging to the three. There they would attempt to meet him and Lady on their return from the holdup.

With these agreements completed, Billy English waited for no more; but, since his was the greatest distance to be covered to reach the railroad he spurred off into the whirling snow, bending his head to the storm.

"Will he make it?" asked Jack Turner anxiously.

"He's got one chance in four, I figure," said The Dean, "of getting there and finding that a guard ain't riding on that platform."

"And if there is a guard, that finishes it?"

"If there's a guard, he's got one chance in a thousand."

"Well," said Jack Turner, "all my life I've been betting on long chances, and I ain't going to stop now. We'll start for Jeffrey Pass."

But already Billy English had forgotten about the work before him and the men behind him. He was entirely occupied in the battle with the storm, with the snow sometimes hurtling into his face in drifts, half choking him.

An hour later the wind abated, and the fall of snow with it. He continued over a country where the snow was swept nearly clean from all level places, but where it had banked and slipped on every slope of any size.

Sometimes he was able to swing along at a round gallop. Again, he was forced to slacken his pace to a jog, or even to a walk, as he floundered through deep drifts. In the gray of the dawn he reached a small house almost buried in snow.

Here he knocked at the door, and the sole occupant, a trapper, hunter, and small rancher, answered. He recognized Billy English at once, for this was one of the stations which the long riders maintained on the mountain desert, keeping a following by a judicious distribution of money here and there.

Sometimes they maintained posts where they were dreaded, and where the house owner would gladly have supported the law, but where they inspired such fear that men dared not deny them.

137

It happened that this lonely out-dweller was only too glad to see one of the daring rovers approach. His season had been bad indeed, and the stay of Billy English meant both money and news.

Accordingly, he put up the fine horse from which Billy dismounted, and allowed the rider to stretch on the bunk for an hour's unbroken rest. After that Billy rose, shook the sleep out of his head and body, drank the coffee and ate the corn pone and bacon offered to him, and swung into the saddle on the trapper's own horse. A liberal donation followed, and leaving his host grinning and waving behind him, Billy shot away on the fresh mount into the storm.

It was much abated by this time. The sky was still as gray, but very little snow flew in the wind. All the day Billy drove south and east on his journey, and in the dusk he arrived at his destination, saddle-cramped and half dead with continual exposure and the beating of the storm.

He stabled the horse at once, told a simple story to the livery keeper to explain the fact that the horse would be left for several days, and that another man would call for it; and then he paid the man to let him sleep another hour on his bunk.

That hour's rest worked wonders with him, and brought him out into the night at length with only a faint ringing in his ears to remind him of the arduous labors of that long grind through the storm.

There was still a full twenty minutes left before the train was due, and he spent this time in warming himself up and unlimbering the muscles of arms and legs with exercise in the cold night.

At length the pulses were pounding through his body; his eye was clear, his hand steady. It was the perfect state of mind and body for the work which lay before him, and now, far down the track, the whistle of the train was caught up by the face of the hill and echoed faintly down the wind.

Billy stayed back from the busy little lighted station as the great headlight poured down the track, caught the station house in a glowing circle, and then, as the engine turned a slight curve, wavered away and plunged down the gleaming rails. It roared closer, stopped, panting steam, instinct with strength; for nothing made by man is so nearly living as a railroad locomotive.

The brief stop was already terminated, and the shack, or brakeman, had swung onto the blind baggage with his lantern. Plainly, they were guarding carefully against hobos, at least. The train began to move, the engine snorting like a horse at the grade and the load it was required to set in motion.

In the meantime, Billy had edged along the track. He must get a sufficient distance ahead, and yet he must not go so far that the spreading circle of the headlight would glow on him. With enough ground between him and the engine, he must wait until, as the train gathered headway, the shack swung down from the blind baggage and stepped onto the train again farther down.

All the time Billy blessed his lucky stars that no guard was riding that same blind baggage, for certainly the shack would not be wasting his time in this fashion if the blind baggage platform were already occupied.

All that could prevent him from getting on, it seemed, would be the ability of the brakeman to stay on that platform for so long, while the train gathered headway, that Billy could not reach the step and handrail as the car flashed past. But this was made the less likely because the shack had to dismount from the platform himself and swing onto the train farther down the line, unless he wished a long and cold ride to the next stopping point.

Accordingly, Billy jogged on, looking over his shoulder as the train gathered headway, and waiting for that moment when he should see the descending arc of light which meant that the shack was swinging down with his lantern.

Now the light showed, hung a moment as the braky waited on the lowest step scanning the track ahead and letting the ground skim beneath his dangling foot. Then he dropped off, the yellow spot of lantern light staggered, and presently it hooked up into the train farther down as the braky swung aboard.

Exultation began to rise in the breast of Billy. That shack, he told himself, was a "simp." In the meantime, the train was advancing at a good round gait, but it was as nothing to him. Taught in the first place by the celebrated King Charlie himself, and so initiated into many fine points of the game, he had improved his opportunities to learn during the past year — or, rather, during his six months of liberty of the past year — and now he was as active and daring in his manipulations around a train as the most expert shack or experienced hobo.

He increased his run to a sprint as the engine thundered past him. Then he faced in and leaped for the handrail of the blind baggage, bunching his feet well up toward his hands to strike out for the step in the darkness.

Fair and true both hands and feet struck. The resulting wrench to the side would have torn a less experienced hand away, but Billy English had allowed himself to sway in, jerking himself closer to the car.

He slipped his hand higher on the handrail — and a heavy blow descended on the fingers, crushing them against the iron! His fingers, numbed by that blow, slid helplessly from the rail, and he lurched to the side, falling. Such a fall meant perhaps a roll under the wheels and horrible mangling — at least a broken neck — as he struck the gravel roadbed.

In the split part of a second which that lurch occupied, he nevertheless had ample time to think of both possibilities. With his right hand he clutched. It struck the rail with stinging impact as he shot to the side. And his grip slipped — held! At the same time he hooked his right foot in, and it caught on the lowest portion of the rail.

In the meantime, the sweep of the train had flattened him against the side of the car, and the only parts of him which even touched the rail or the steps were the extended right hand and the foot. No wonder, then, that the man who had delivered the blow, now looking down, saw nothing and shouted fiercely into the night.

"One cursed hobo less in the world!"

The words shrieked with inhuman loudness in the ear of Billy.

So the platform, after all, was guarded! If he swung back onto the steps, he would be beaten off them by an armed man, for no doubt that blow had been delivered with a revolver butt. To be sure, if he swung back quickly enough, he might be able to get into his place on the steps, jerk out his revolver, and kill the shadowy form above him.

But Billy English had never yet shot to kill, and that thought was impossible for him. Nevertheless, he could not hang there indefinitely, with the wind tugging at him. He held on until the fingers of his injured hand commenced to ache.

Then he drew himself back, cringing down and making himself small on the lowest step, and peering up in an anguish, half expectant of seeing the dull glimmer of raw steel in the night above him.

But no. He could see the vague shadow of the brakeman's body as the fellow stood guard, but apparently there was no motion. He had dismissed all thought of Billy from his mind. To him it was impossible that Billy should be alive. His thoughts must be picturing the tramp crushed beneath the whirring wheels of the long train, or else smashed on the roadbed where he might have fallen.

What a malignantly cruel trap it had been to have the brakeman swing on and off, and, all the time with the platform guarded!

Hot rage mastered Billy English and made him shake for an instant. That was his greatest enemy, that blind rage which leaped on him and blurred his eyes with red. He shook the passion off instantly, and, cold and ready for action, gripping his smashed left hand, in spite of the pain, around the handrail, he slipped up, changed his footing, then dived over the top of the steps and at the knees of the guard, shooting himself in with the full strength of his arms and with a lucky sway of the train to drive him all the faster.

He succeeded so very well that he nearly rolled them both to a horrible death on the far side. The shack went down like lead, too stunned by surprise even to shriek, and he and Billy tumbled to the very verge of the far steps. Both clutched for safety in the nick of time. But as they scrambled back, Billy chopped down with his clenched right hand, and hard knuckles thudded home just under the ear of his enemy.

The shack stretched out limp, without a murmur, and Billy set about calmly binding the hands and feet of the victim. After that, he went through the pockets of his man, extracted and restored the wallet — there was none of the petty thief in Billy — and at length wound up by taking the fellow's gun and knife and tossing them into the darkness.

CHAPTER XIX

WHEN THE TRAIN STOPPED

As the train lurched forward, still gaining speed on the grade, Billy English settled back, crouching on his heels, and attempted to examine his injured hand; but in the darkness that was impossible.

There arose in him a singular feeling of fierce triumph. Since that blow which the shack had given him by surprise, he felt that whatever he might do would be simply an act of retaliation. Behind him the long train was thundering, each car loaded with life, gayety, unconcern. Before him the engine labored swiftly up the rails. And all of this power and the cargo it was transporting might be stopped and held still by his sole command. No wonder that it set him breathing deeply.

But suppose, when he climbed over the tender, that the engineer and his fireman showed fight? They were a hardy lot, these trainmen, used to danger and the taking of chances, and trained to consider their own lives as nothing compared with the comfort and safety of the passengers in their charge. Suppose they were to attack him in spite of the drawn revolver which he leveled at them? A warm trickle was dripping down his fingers, and when they saw this, they might be the more

144

encouraged to attack him. In that case, what could he do?

The resolution which was so deeply implanted in him — that he would never shoot to kill, least of all a harmless, law-abiding citizen — had become worse than a gun pointed at his head. What was the taking of a common chance to other bandits, became a mortal peril to him. But he drew his revolver and felt some consolation as the roughened butt pressed up into the palm of his hand.

In the meantime, the shack was wakening. He had been badly laid out by that blow beneath the ear, driven home with such cruel force; now he roused himself with a groan, and there was a fierce and silent struggle as he strove to free himself from the bonds.

Billy English watched and listened without a word, for he enjoyed the spectacle immensely, there on that black-shadowed blind baggage. There is no love wasted between the brakemen and any of the criminal class who are forced to travel by stealth on the railroads. They hate one another heartily, and take advantage of any opening to inflict pain on their enemies. If there is an occasional friendly shack, the root of his friendliness is usually found in his belief that he can extract a few dollars from the hobo for the passage on that division.

These two, therefore, glared at each other through the darkness. The shack was only astonished to find that he had not been tumbled from the platform to die wretchedly on the roadbed as

145

he fell. He decided, therefore, that he was being reserved for some finer torture, and he began to shout as soon as his wriggling had revealed the fact that he was securely tied, hand and foot. Strips of his own clothes had been used to make those bonds.

The shouting was stopped by a hand which shot under his chin and secured a strong grip on his throat.

He heard a voice mutter: "You damned shack, I'll tear your head off if you let out another yap!"

He lay still. In the first place, the voice was convincing in intonation. In the second place, the finger tips which had gripped at his throat were like tearing steel. He saw that it would be well to consider this game concluded. Now the cold muzzle of a revolver was shoved into his face.

"I'd blow you to eternity, shack," said Billy English, "if it wasn't easier and quicker, almost, just to roll you off the train and let the ground hit you. That'd be sure enough, the way we're shooting. But you lie still, and maybe you'll come through this, yet! I ain't promising, understand? But I won't bump you off unless you get to really bothering me!"

The brakeman lay still as death. He was a brave man. He had been picked for the cold duty of guarding the blind baggage for that reason, and for his relentless hatred of tramps. But now he realized that a life which he had really lost was being restored to him, and he neither stirred nor spoke.

"When in doubt, keep your mouth shut." This is a great law of the road.

Billy English settled back again and watched the mountains growing up on either hand. The wind had whisked the heavens clean of clouds, and now the sky was mottled with points of fire, a stippled background against which the dark peaks were in relief. They rose higher and higher. They crowded closer, until it seemed that at length they would close above the rushing train; and Billy English knew that they were nearing Jeffrey Pass.

He began to grow tense as the time for action approached. He slipped down on the steps and swung out. He could mark the place well. Straight ahead rose the great sugar-loaf mountain which was to be his milestone.

Back he clambered, went up the back of the tender with great agility in spite of his crippled, aching hand, and from the top turned and snarled a warning back at the shack, who was cursing softly in the realization that his conqueror was something more than an ordinary tramp.

"If you open your head," snapped Billy English, "I'll stop what I'm doing and come back here and slice your throat, you rat! Keep thinking about that!"

The shack was silenced. Billy turned and resumed his progress. A second later he was peering at the engineer's back as he leaned against the side of the cab to stare down the tracks. Just then the heart of Billy smote him. There was so much weariness and yet honest purpose combined in the grease-marked, overall-clad back of the engineer that Billy almost relented.

Above him the sugar-loaf was thrusting higher and higher into the heavens. Somewhere on the far side of it, Jack Turner — the great Jack Turner himself! — and The Dean and Joe Hoyt, every one of them a man in a million, crouched in waiting. They had made out the roar of the train in this narrow pass long before they saw the headlight; but now it must be playing down the rails as it turned the last curve. And those men who waited were wondering if he, Billy English, would play his part.

It was no little thing. To have stopped such a train would entitle him to deathless consideration among their ranks. He would become a known man, one of those the mention of whose name caused the other dwellers in the underworld to lift their brows in attention and respect.

And yet such a consideration was no consideration at all. Yonder in the mountains somewhere King Charlie had driven with his buckboard and carried the Lady girl to a new refuge. Yonder in the mountains they were waiting for the return.

"This is the last time!" panted Billy to himself. "After this there won't be no call for such things. I can put her up like the little lady she is. I can fix her so that she can live in style. I can give her everything that I missed!"

His big, generous boy's heart swelled with the resolve.

An instant later he was in the cab with his

wounded hand doubled to conceal its injury. His leveled revolver was as steady as though rested upon a rock.

"All right, boys," he said quietly. "You don't have to shove your hands up. Just watch that you don't make any fast move. Understand? I ain't going to wait to see where you move your hands. But as soon as you let a hand jump, I'm going to shoot."

He had learned the greatest lesson that any criminal can learn, and that is, when confronting a victim, to keep on thinking, not to attempt to bluff the other, but to let him become aware of a coldly sure and active brain at work. As he had slipped on his mask before climbing onto the tender, he had steadied himself for the part which he must play. Now he was instantly at home in it.

The fireman was a youth of twenty-five, with the red hair and the fighting blue eyes of an Irishman. He leaned against the side of the cab and glared at Billy with deathless hate. As for the engineer, he seemed dazed. He even forgot himself so far as to make one of the quick motions against which Billy had cautioned him — but the movement was up — a flicker of the hand across his face. He seemed to be brushing a mist from his eyes.

Billy would have thought him drunk, had he not seen him at his post. He was not drunk. He was simply dazed at the catastrophe which was befalling, not him, but the train which was under his charge.

"You'll stop up yonder the minute you get past the sugar-loaf, friend," said Billy English.

He was hoping that the young fireman with the fighting face had not noticed that he was allowing the move of the hand to go for nothing. Once either of them decided that there was the slightest element of a bluff about this holdup, Billy knew that he would have them both at his throat in deadly earnest.

"You'd better begin easing up on this train," said Billy.

The engineer merely stared, his forehead wrinkling as though there were no comprehension in his brain. And then he lurched at Billy with arms outspread. He was a big man — a full two hundred pounds, and though he must have been well past forty, he was still strong with muscle under the outer layer of fat. Billy English saw the Irishman, with a hoarse shout of battle rage, gather himself to leap in to the assistance of his comrade, regardless of the fact that the revolver was pointed full in his face.

Even in that crisis Billy admired their courage with all his boyish, quick heart. He had six deaths there under his trigger finger. But he could not shoot any more than if his hand had been paralyzed. Instead, he jerked back the revolver and struck sideways with it, cutting the engineer along the head with the long, heavy barrel of the gun. There was a thud of the steel sinking into the bone, and the big man went down while the fireman was stopped, with his hands at the very throat of Billy, by the feel of the revolver muzzle as it was jabbed into his abdomen. For an instant he hesitated. Then he gave way to the inevitable, and fell back.

"He ain't dead," said Billy, answering the despairing look which the fireman cast at his late chief. "He's just knocked cold. Now, curse you, stop this train, or I'll stop you first and the train afterward."

With a groan the fireman turned. The fall of the engineer had had some weight with him. He worked for a moment; then Billy saw a small cloud of steam roll into the cab, and an instant later the engine stopped chugging and the brakes began to grind, catching on the whole length of the train.

To the right, the great sugar-loaf drifted past with diminishing speed. But what if he stopped the train too soon? What if, when it halted and the train crew poured out to learn the reason for the halt, his comrades were not present? In that case he would be immediately swamped. But for that he could only trust to chance. Jack Turner would not be apt to let his share of such a bargain fall through unaccomplished.

The engine rocked, halted with a jar, and Billy backed down onto the step, hooking his left arm through the rail to steady himself, because his left hand was now so swollen and painful that he could not grip with it.

Here he waited. Down the train he heard voices, and the noise of traps being jerked up.

Then, like a blessing to his straining ears, came

the voice of Joe Hoyt booming from the darkness just at his side: "Good work! Good work, pal! Make 'em flood the fire box, now."

Billy heard a man running past, with another behind. Hoyt and another were taking that side of the train. He heard the voice of The Dean shouting on the far side of the train, "Keep inside, folks. We ain't aiming to harm nobody. Just keep inside them cars."

Here the engineer heaved himself to his elbow with a groan.

"Oh, Lord," he was muttering, "I'd rather have died. It's the first accident in twenty years. It's the first time, Mike, that my train has been stopped by —"

"Shut up!" cut in Billy, as much to stop the progress of his own sympathy for the man as to get action. "Shut up! This fire box has to be flooded. Get busy, boys!"

Unless this were done, the train would thunder on out of the pass and in a few minutes, from the nearest station, the telegraph wires would be charged with messages rousing the whole district against the outlaws. The leveled revolver forced both the engineer and the fireman to do as Billy English commanded. Those other voices in the night made Billy seem a more important figure.

Hoyt and Jack Turner and The Dean were shouting back and forth with loud clamors. The Dean in particular was running hither and yon, so that at one instant he was shouting from one end of the train, and at another from a quite different section. The air was filled with voices. Had he not known the actual number, Billy would have thought that a score were engaged in the holdup. He caught other noises — the shrill cry of a terrified woman, and then two sharp reports of a revolver, followed by the heavy roar of what Billy knew must be a sawed-off shotgun.

What had happened there? He had no chance to think. The roar of the steam as the water was turned into the fire box drowned his very capacity for thought and emotion.

Then he stepped back from the engine. There was no longer need to watch the engine crew since the engine was dead. There was a greater need for him to see if his companions did not require his aid farther down the train. Either one of them was dead or wounded, or one of the train crew was down — or had that roar of the shotgun proved to be simply a blind effort at resistance?

He found the latter to be the case. The men who were guarding the money shipment had been routed out of their stronghold by the roared threat of Jack Turner that he would use enough "soup" to blow both the car and its contents to the devil unless they opened the door.

They had taken him at his word, and, opening the door, they had leaped out, both of them, with shotguns ready. But before they could locate their enemies, Joe Hoyt, from the side, had fired low and brought them both down with snap shots, aimed low. Wounded through the legs, they had dropped to the ground, and there one of them,

153

in pain and despair had fired both barrels of his gun blindly.

No harm was done to the robbers, and an instant later Jack Turner was in the car and at work on the safe.

These facts were briefly communicated to Billy by Joe Hoyt as the two guards sat up and worked at bandaging their wounds and strewing curses through the air.

"What can I do now?" asked Billy.

"Start praying, kid," muttered Hoyt. "Just start praying that these blockheads don't find out that there ain't about a million of us. I wish that there was ten Turners in there working to blow the safe. Every second counts for us. Here he comes!"

Jack Turner swung out of the black doorway of the car and ran toward them.

"Get these out of the way!" commanded Turner. The two guards were seized and dragged several paces before Turner commanded: "Now get down on the ground — flat!"

They dropped, and hardly had they done so when there was the sound of the explosion, not like thunder, but like an immense puff of air; if such a thing can be imagined, multiplied a thousandfold. At the same time there was a sort of soft blow that shook Billy from head to foot. Looking sidewise, he saw the top of the car lift as though on hinges and settle back with a great crash.

Jack Turner was on his feet already and running with peculiar speed, in spite of his limp. Into the car he leaped. And then suddenly they heard a wail of rage from him. He jumped down at once, stamping and raving and beating his hands together like one possessed.

"What's up?" cried Hoyt. "Was it an empty?"

"It's a double safe!" cried Turner. "I peeled the outside off like a shell but —" His voice died in curses.

He was able to gasp out at length: "And there ain't a drop of soup left! I've used it all up in the first try!"

CHAPTER XX

TO BE WORTHY

By simple processes, the minds of the great bring the defeat of their enemies; and, by simple neglect of little things, they themselves are destroyed. Napoleon was beaten at Waterloo by indigestion, not by the red-coated squares against which the French cavalry ground itself to pieces. And yet the mind of Billy English grasped at, but could not comprehend, the fact that the great Jack Turner, of whom he had heard in his very childhood, should have played so amateur a prank as to use up all of his soup in blasting the outer jacket off the safe.

But the realization of what had happened was now brought home to them sharply. Far down the length of the train a number of men poured out from a car, and there was a sudden fusillade of shots that hummed and whirred around the heads of the robbers. They could stand their ground and drive these fellows back, perhaps, with a few well-directed shots; but what was there to be gained by fighting?

Jack Turner whistled loud and shrill, and set the example by turning about and bolting for the brush. Joe Hoyt did likewise. But what of The

Dean, left unsuccored on the far side of the train?

Billy English called to his companions to stay and hold back the crowd until The Dean had secured his retreat. But they made no answer. He then dropped to the ground and tried the effect of a few well-directed shots sent into the air, but close enough to the heads of the passengers for them to hear the whine of the bullets.

The result was magic. Down dropped the advancing line of half a dozen bold spirits. They sent a fierce fusillade, which whizzed above the spot where Billy lay breast high. He was amusing himself with shooting out the windows of the cars, with a resultant crash of glass that kept back the armed men of several other coaches.

But suddenly the whole train seemed to waken to the fact that yonder in the dimness there was only a single man opposing them. Wild yells of rage tore the night, and men bolted out from every car.

As for Billy, he had accomplished his purpose. In the interim The Dean had raced for the head of the train on the farther side. Now Billy saw what he had been straining his eyes to observe — a tall, spare figure leaping around the front of the engine and breaking for the dense woods. Billy himself followed with all speed.

They had delayed not a second for the sake of The Dean. And even for Billy they were waiting only a moment. They were just urging their horses away when he burst upon them and leaped without a word upon the back of the spare mount. Well he knew the feel of the good chestnut's barrel between his knees! He flung himself forward along the neck of the horse, like the others, and instantly they were shooting ahead parallel with the railroad, but screened from it, for a hundred yards, by the narrow row of trees.

Shots of the enraged men from the train combed the trees above their heads; but, when they emerged from shelter far down the pass, they were effectually screened by the darkness, and began to draw their horses into a more moderate gait.

Here The Dean pulled his horse in to the side of Billy.

"Waiting for me like that was a pretty white thing to do, son," he said. "I'll remember."

"Aw, the devil," growled Billy. "Don't talk about it. You'd do the same for me."

Through the night they rode on, with never a word spoken concerning their disappointment. They climbed through the first range of the mountains and, when they had circled down into easier ground beyond, Jack Turner drew in his rein.

"I'm going to leave you boys here. I'll have to owe you this hoss, though."

"Keep him, Jack," they told him. "You're welcome."

"Because I'm broke," he persisted. "But I'll be flush again one of these days, and I'll have another idea. Then I'll come and hunt you boys up — unless you've decided that you don't like the kind of luck that I bring."

They laughed such a thought away. They would

try luck with him any day, they declared. Then he came closer to Billy English and said: "Billy, you done a fine bit of work in stopping that train. I'll tell you something, man to man: I knowed that that train was going to be guarded. But I sent you after the job, anyway. The reason was that I wanted to see what sort of stuff was in you. Well, son, I sure know now what you can do, and you're going to hear from me again one of these days. So long!"

"So long," said Billy, and watched the outlaw turn and ride into the night.

He himself rode downheaded with his companions along the trail which led to their place of rendezvous with King Charlie and Lady.

"That was rare talk to hear from Jack Turner," said The Dean after a time. "He's got about as much warmth in him as a fish."

Billy grunted, as his way was, and continued in his brown study.

Dawn found them far away in the foothills, with six hours to ride before they would reach the rendezvous, and still there was no sign of pursuit behind them. Long before this the telegraph must have been humming with news of their attempt. It had failed, but they had stopped the mails, and they had shot two law-abiding citizens. Moreover, there was something which particularly struck the imagination in a crime which had to do with the stopping of a great train in the mountains by a mere handful of men. No doubt the hills were buzzing with news of them, and every village was sending out its quota to hunt for them.

By one thing alone were they favored. The storm had started again with the first blur of daylight, and now the wind was howling through the hills, bearing thick drifts of the snow before it. Men were not apt to hunt with such zest in this impracticable and discouraging weather. More than that, they would be most likely to have a hard time in discovering any trail of the fugitives.

The last hours of the journey were weary ones. They did not speak at all. They merely swayed with the laboring, leg-weary horses until, at length, they came on the welcome smell of wood-smoke blowing down the wind. In the throat of the narrow gorge, where they had told him to go, they found King Charlie ensconced with Lady.

The little shack had been busily repaired by the old tramp during the day. Now it was fairly storm-tight. On the great, clumsily built hearth at the end of the room there was a big fire of logs blazing, and over this fire simmered scraps of broken pots and pans which Charlie had found, scoured out, and now had filled with various sorts of food.

When they had put up their horses in the shed behind the house and come in, they found Louise Alison Dora Young sitting in the middle of the floor profoundly engaged with a doll, which consisted of a potato with matches stuck into it for arms and legs.

She leaped up with a shout and came running to greet them. Billy English, entering last and closing the door behind him, chuckled as he saw the

160

two big men, stern from their hazardous and profitless adventure, shrug away their gloom and scoop her up into their arms with laughter.

Last of all, she insisted on sitting on the knee of Billy and superintending the job which King Charlie set about cleansing and binding up the battered hand which the brakeman had struck.

The food was served, and they ate as men, who had labored without the comfort of food for eighteen hours, can eat. But more than the food, more than the drowsy, pleasant warmth in the room, more than the kindly face and the soothing voice of the man whom he thought was his father, Billy English centered his attention on the bright head of Lady.

Afterward he drew King Charlie to one side and consulted him seriously in murmurs.

"What would you think," he said, "of doing what I suggested the other day — cutting loose from your trains and your rod-riding and settling down somewhere, where I can look after you and you can look after Lady?"

The old man refilled his pipe and lighted it before he answered.

"Sounds pretty well," he said, "and it might work pretty well — until some gent like Turner come along with a good proposition to break your neck and make a million. Then you'd go off with him just the way you went off this time! Nope, I couldn't put no sort of reliance on you, Billy. And I'd have to be able to put reliance on you before I could think of settling down."

"What's the harm in an experiment?" asked Billy sadly.

"I'll tell you what's the harm. A traveling gent like me needs to have a pretty thick skin and a hard skin. I've got both them things by just rolling along and never stopping. But if I was to settle down, it would only be a day or two before I lost all my calluses, so to speak. And then where would I be when you left me again? I'd be just as helpless as if I'd never learned nothing about how to take care of myself."

Billy English shook his head. "I'll never leave you again," he said solemnly.

"Make me believe that."

"I can. Look at the girl."

"I been looking at nothing else for the whole day, until you boys come in."

"Well, look again. She's worth it. When I look at her, I understand that she is a lady, and that the only way I can hope to take care of her is to be a gentleman. Understand? So I'm going to make myself over."

"H'm," said King Charlie. "Seems to me that I've heard long riders talk like that before."

"This time," said Billy, "you're hearing one that means it. Why, look at her, and tell me if she ain't a lady! And if she is, how am I ever going to give her the proper sort of a bringing up unless I make myself decent? Look at her, King!"

And King Charlie looked and looked, and at length removed his pipe and stared with dim, sad eyes at the child.

CHAPTER XXI

A ROYAL RETREAT

PANGS of hunger beset King Charlie, and there was an odd weakness just behind each knee, the sure sign that he had fasted long. Yet he maintained his dignity as he strolled down the street, even as befitted one with the nickname of royalty. He cast no furtive and hunted glances from side to side. There was no half-cringing and half-snarling appeal in his manner. Instead, he walked on slowly, with the easy air of a man of leisure, now and again pausing to glance in at the windows, for he was on the main street of the little town of Culver Crossing, and the chief stores lay compactly within the next two blocks.

But when he turned his face to look at the windows, he was not observing their contents. He was merely studying the reflections of passing faces in the heavy plate glass. He was noting a score of people at a glance, perhaps, and striving to select a victim. If King Charlie was to eat, some one must proffer the means out of his pocketbook.

As for getting a meal by "battering doors," there was no hope. For a day and a half he had fondly nursed the delusion that somewhere in Culver Crossing he would be able to find a soft heart and

163

a well-stocked kitchen. But not long before some "tramp-royals," with smiling faces and fine "fronts," had passed through that little Western town, robbing by night the houses from which they begged meals during the day. Accordingly The King found hard looks from the women and threatening fists from the husbands. And there were no meals.

Even the perpetual color which flared in the midst of his weather-tinted cheeks, and which no danger, no fatigue could greatly dim, was now beginning to wane. It was like the dying flame of a candle. It showed how close the high spirits of the tramp were to dark extinction. And though he still carried his sixty-odd years with a light step and a casual demeanor, King Charlie was rapidly growing desperate.

It was just at this moment, when he turned from the window of Culver Crossing's leading haberdashery, that he saw his first good opening, and this opening was more than good. It was a gift from Heaven, he felt, and afforded a vision of square meals for an indefinite period.

What he saw was a wallet which had been drawn from an inside coat pocket by a wide-shouldered man just ahead of him. After a glance at the contents, accompanied by the crisp rustling of the wind down the edges of many bills, the man had dropped it into an outside pocket of his overcoat.

King Charlie reached for the surface of the plate-glass window and supported himself. It was like having a fortune placed in his hand by the will of a dead relative, so secure would this be. Instantly he froze to the man of the wallet. The fellow was well dressed, though rather flashy in his choice of colors. He even wore a cane, which gave him a foreign and, it seemed to King Charlie, a rather distinguished air. He was very tall, and he was as lean as he was tall, and the gloved hand which swung at his side, showed fingers of amazing length.

Altogether there was something entirely strange and yet something oddly familiar about his make-up, and King Charlie did his best to identify in his mind the recollection of the man. Since the other never turned, however, The King did not succeed in his effort, and he gave up the attempt at once when he saw the hand, which had dropped into the overcoat pocket with the wallet, come out without it.

Truly the fellow must be a foreigner. It was bad enough to swing a cane and wear gloves, and thereby focus all eyes upon him as he strode down the street of Culver Crossing. It was still worse to leave a wallet in an outside overcoat pocket on this windy, chill, October day.

Slipping up closely to the stranger, King Charlie waited until the tall man was merged in a knot of pedestrians waiting for a hay wagon to pass at a street crossing, and then, when all the eyes in the crowd were drawn up, as the driver of the wagon on his lofty seat made some remark, King Charlie dipped his hand into the pocket.

Once that hand had been famous for its skill.

Even now that he was an old man, he could do certain things with a delicate deftness which a youth with the sensitive fingers of a musician might have envied. Down inside the flap of the coat the fingers stole. They glided down with equal caution and speed. They encountered the upstanding stem of a pipe which had been placed in the pocket. They passed this, and the tips rubbed over the rough surface of the old leather wallet.

Down hooked the little finger until it was under the lowest part of the wallet, and then he began to withdraw the prize slowly, making sure that a sudden diminution of the weight in his pocket should not attract the attention of the tall, slender victim.

At length the wallet was near the top of the pocket; then, with a movement of consummate speed and smoothness, the wallet was transferred from the pocket of the victim to his own inside breast pocket. The whole operation had been a single deft insertion and withdrawal of the hand.

Now The King drew back and stepped to the side, working through the knot of people toward the side street, while the little group, released by the passing of the wagon and its load of baled hay, surged on over the crossing.

Turning back to the right, King Charlie paused at the side window of the store he had just passed. In the first place he did not wish to draw attention to himself by hurry; in the second place he did not wish to isolate himself from the pedestrians along the main street by going down this alley.

A crowd meant safety.

Moreover, in the reflection in that window, he could dimly follow the movements of the tall man. The latter crossed the street with the rest, but, when he reached the opposite curb, he paused and whirled sharply, and as he whirled, even in the wavering and uncertain reflection in the window, The King recognized his man.

Blockhead, treble fool that he had been! There were revealed to him the long face and the many-wrinkled features of The Dean, that famous gambler and terrible gun fighter. The Dean! Had he not chummed with that man in the long distant past? Had he not known The Dean as a fellow trencherman at the same table? Had they not entered upon the same exploits together? Were they not mutual friends of Billy English of strange and wonderful memory? Yes, this was the man, and hardly changed by the ten years which had elapsed since The King last saw him.

Why, under the wide blue heavens, had not King Charlie recognized him? If he had struck The Dean while flush, as he was now, The Dean at the least would have forked over twenty dollars, and that meant comparative comfort until he had beaten his way out of the West, where only laborers flourished, back to the East, where a dyed-in-the-wool one would be given a chance. But, like a fool, he had helped himself, and now the chances were even that he would draw a grim vengeance upon his head. Or should he simply go back to The Dean and tell him what had happened and apologize for having taken the wallet of a man whom he had not recognized? No, that would be a thin excuse to so sharp a fellow as the tall gambler.

But while The King paused, full of an agony of doubts, The Dean began striding back across the street, searching every face, with eyes as glittering and keen as the eyes of a snake. His right hand was dropped inside the breast of his coat, and well The King knew that the long, bony fingers of his former companion were wrapped around the handle of a revolver, and if that revolver were drawn, it would probably lodge a bullet in The King's poor flesh!

Should he await the nearer approach of the tall man? In spite of the fact that he knew it would be much the wiser thing simply to stand there and stare through the window at the display, he could not help flinching. With his best air of nonchalance he thrust his hands into his trouser pockets and, turning down the alley, began to saunter away.

Instantly he saw that he had done wrong. To thrust hands into his pockets was far too youthful a means of showing an idle disposition for a man of his years. Moreover who would wish to saunter down the alley? He should rather have stepped out at a brisk pace.

A footfall crunched on the gravel of the walk behind him, and panic struck through the soul of The King. He started forward at a quickened pace. Then, in spite of his endeavor, he could not help throwing a glance over his shoulder, and that glance showed him that The Dean had not stirred in pursuit!

No, he was standing irresolute on the corner. It was a young boy who had come a few paces down to look in the window. But the moment The Dean caught sight of that furtive glance he was hot on the trail. With a brief, deep shout he snatched the revolver from its hiding place in his coat.

"Stop, thief!" he thundered.

King Charlie lunged forward, as if about to take to his heels. But his second step was a spring to the side, which flattened him against the wall of the house. At the same instant the revolver exploded, and the bullet literally brushed past his face. His maneuver had saved him by a hair's breadth from the first aimed shot, which, as is known, is apt to be the most accurate shot fired from a revolver.

The instant that shot whirred past him, King Charlie was off again racing like a youngster of twenty years. He kept dodging as he ran, and that veering course was enough to save him from the four shots which the tall man pumped down the alley, the noise of one crowding the echoes of the preceding. Then, with a yell, The Dean raced in pursuit, and behind him a dozen quickly gathered recruits hurried.

Obviously that race could not last long, as The Dean well knew. King Charlie was old. Terror had, to be sure, poured a false strength into his limbs, but that strength was already ebbing and

169

leaving him his original age-numbed muscles. Inside of three minutes at the most the powerful hand of The Dean would fasten upon him, unless the latter chose to shoot him down at short range, as he came up.

All of this was in the quick-working brain of King Charlie as he swerved out onto the narrow street beyond. And there good fortune once more helped him, for at that moment he saw a buggy driven up the street, with a boy in the seat.

With a groan of joy The King flew for the rig and, as the boy drew up the reins with a startled exclamation, flung himself into the seat and tore the strips of leather from the hands of the driver. The latter showed fight, but he was deterred by the sight of the blue-nosed revolver which The King shoved into his ribs.

"Get out that whip," said The King, "and start flogging that horse. We got to be traveling, son, and we need a fast start!"

Now the pursuit, headed by the flying form of The Dean, plunged out of the alley and started up a Babel in the street. A yell of rage and despair came from the lips of the tall gambler, and he saw the position of the thief. Then the whip descended with a loud crack along the back of the horse, which spurted ahead at a full gallop.

It was not a very fast horse nor a very young one, but that first detour to the side of the main street gave The King a priceless handicap, for it led the pursuers away from their horses. They had to stop and turn back for the means of carrying on the pursuit, and in the meantime The King had made hay, while the perilous sun shone. The buggy bumped out at the lower end of the town, and The King found himself driving among the hills.

A gathering roar of horses' hoofs and shouting men's voices in the rear told that the impromptu posse had formed and was spurring to get on his traces.

"Say, where's the main-line railroad, kid?" he asked the trembling boy.

"Two mile ahead."

"Fine! Now you jump!"

"Not while the rig's going like this? Why, it'll kill me, mister!"

"Get up!" He prodded the boy up with the muzzle of his gun. He dared not slow down for the sake of the boy, but at the same time he must not let the youngster follow him and his plans. And the absence of his weight from the buggy might make a vital difference before the race was over. "Jump!"

With a wail of dismay the boy threw up his arms and leaped into the air. Luckily he landed in thick, deep dust which had the effect of muffling his shout. At the end of his roll he came to his feet unhurt, a white form, and shouted hatred and defiance after The King.

CHAPTER XXII

THE KING'S FAREWELL

THE latter had put the whip to the horse and was rollicking up the road at a terrific gait, the buggy flying up at every bump which they crossed. Looking back, as he neared the top of the rise, he saw the horsemen issuing from the town in a dense group, which rapidly lengthened out, as the fastest horses took the lead and began to draw away from the rest.

Conspicuous among the rest he saw The Dean. By the length of that gaunt body he could tell him. From some cow-puncher in the town the gambler had borrowed a speedy mount. He had thrown away his overcoat. His hat had been blown from his head. He rode with his revolver naked and flashing in his hand, and he yelled like a madman, at the very head of the procession.

Plainly he meant business. And The King knew perfectly well what The Dean in a serious mood was capable of. No Indian could be more cruel, no giant could show greater strength.

Again he turned to the whipping of the horse. The ground from this high point sloped rapidly down, and so they gained impetus at every leap. And ahead of him he saw a streak of dim light, the tracks of the railroad, a scant mile away. Not only were the tracks of the railroad visible, but the noise of a train was rumbling nearer and nearer among the hills. Oh, to be on that train and hurtling away!

But the pace of his horse was growing perceptibly slower now, and the poor nag was showing a lameness in the right forefoot. The King, with a yell of despair, stood up to apply the whip with greater effect. As he did so, the tall form of The Dean loomed above the hilltop behind him and exploded his revolver. A random bullet whistled after the fugitive, merely by way of showing him that the chase would be a hot one.

And hot and short it certainly promised to be. Desperately The King turned over chances in his mind. But, even if he were to throw away that well-stuffed wallet, it made no difference. He would be arrested for carrying a concealed weapon and for stealing a horse, which was a serious crime in this part of the country, and for various and sundry other offenses.

Naturally the horsemen were gaining — gaining fast. All he could do was to keep on at the best speed he could make and trust to luck that something could happen. But what could happen? They would have run down the horse and buggy within a few minutes. And they were too close for him to attempt to leave the buggy and hide himself in some gully among the hills.

Then, startlingly near, he saw a misty cloud of smoke rising and sweeping closer and closer. It was the smoke and vapor from an engine laboring up the grade through the hills. As he rounded another hill, The King saw the train itself, the engine sweeping grandly about a curve, as it thundered into view.

King Charlie's heart went out to it. There was his kingdom, there was his country — the land of the metal rails — which twine together in the dwindling distance, the land of freight and passenger expresses and the empty box cars! Oh, to be on it! The stately freight was empty. Even at this distance he could tell that by the sound of rattling which the cars made as they poured up the track. If he were on that train he would wish for only one thing — that the train were going east instead of west!

But could he not reach the train? At least it was his only hope to reach that train and so be drawn away from the pursuit. He knew trainmen well, but no engineer would stop his train on such a slope and break up his running schedule for the sake of a mere thief.

He stood up in the buggy again and called aloud upon the poor horse which labored between the shafts, pounding its forefeet to ruin, as it galloped down the slope, and the wretched animal seemed to know the need and responded to it with a greater burst of speed. Instinctively The King knew that the whip could not draw from the horse more than it was already giving, so he dropped it and looked back to see what progress The Dean and the others were making.

They were coming up fast enough, but they could have come faster. He could see the face of The Dean quite clearly now, and it was no longer the face of a man in a frenzy. No doubt he had seen that the chase could have only one ending, and he was in no hurry to bring about that conclusion. He would rather draw out the misery of the fugitive. So he had put away his revolver and was drawing up his horse and letting the rest of the posse catch up with him.

King Charlie, with a groan, turned to look toward the train. It was running slowly, comparatively speaking, but no horse could keep up for any distance with even the speed which it maintained upon the grade. But it seemed to The King that he had the ghost of a chance. At least he could thank Heaven that The Dean did not see and understand his purpose. Otherwise the tall gambler would have spurred in upon him, and the chase would even now be over.

But the latter still held back. It was only when the train was passing across the road, not a furlong away, that The Dean saw and understood. And as he saw he yelled to his mount and leaned forward to bring it again to its full speed.

The distance was too short, however, to make up much vital ground. The old horse whipped the buggy forward at a flying pace, and now The King turned from the road and close beside the speeding train was whipping up the track beside the box cars.

Rapidly they drifted past him. The engine was

gaining speed with every instant, as, reaching a level stretch, the drain of the upgrade diminished. Then The King saw the thing for which he had been praying, a smooth stretch where he could swing the buggy in close to the edge of the ties.

He yelled to the horse and gave a final cut to rouse that poor animal to yet more frantic efforts. Then he climbed back over the seat and stood up on the edge of the sideboard. The side of the box car was like a lofty wall hurtling past him.

A wild yell and the explosion of firearms caused him to glance to the side, and there he saw The Dean flogging his horse with a quirt in his left hand, while he blazed away with the revolver in his right.

Now King Charlie picked out the first iron ladder that whirled past him and leaped for it. Fair and true his feet and his hands struck the rounds. A moment later he lay flat on the top of the car, gasping and panting for breath, while the bullets purred over his head. Presently he looked back and saw The Dean spurring his horse down the track.

Just too late the tall fellow had solved the plan of The King and had taken to the pursuit. He had swung off the highway and onto the roadbed of the train just too late, for the last car of the train was drawing past.

For a minute he raced his horse after the train and gained a trifle on it, but at the end of a hundred yards the pace told, and the mustang began to fall back, while the train gathered more and more speed. It was then that King Charlie rose to his feet. He took off the hat which had not been displaced in spite of all his gymnastic endeavors of the past few minutes, and he waved that hat at The Dean and gave him a rousing shout of mockery and farewell.

At the same minute a hand fell on his shoulder. He turned quickly and found himself looking into the face of a hardy young brakeman, athletic of build, solid of shoulder, red of hair. On the whole he was exactly the sort of "shack" that even the hardiest of tramps would not care to have trouble with. But now the youngster grinned and nodded at him.

"Say," he exclaimed, "you sure swing a neat pair of heels for an old boy your age. How old are you, bo?"

"Old enough to know better than to lead the sort of a life that I lead," said The King with a mock sadness.

The youthful brakeman laughed with great good-nature.

"What were they after you for?" he asked.

"Just for nothing, if you ask me," said The King with a shrug of the shoulder. "All I did was to look into a gent's coat and lift out a bit of spare paper that was littering up his pocket. And here it is!"

He had folded his arms, and one hand was dipped inside his breast coat pocket and extracted a bill which he then dropped into his side pocket, and this was what he now exposed under the eyes

177

of the brakeman. The latter exploded a single great curse.

"Did they raise all that noise on account of that?"

It was a one-dollar bill which fluttered in the stream of air.

"Son, you don't know Culver Crossing," said The King sadly. "They started after me not on account of that one dollar, but because of the principle of the thing. That's the kind of a town it is! I been battering doors for two days trying to get a hand-out. And nary a bit of food have I had!"

The brakeman swore again in sympathy.

"Well," he said, "you keep that dollar. I've got the change for it, but I guess you're old enough to need all of the loot that you can get!"

CHAPTER XXIII

THE UNINVITED GUEST

AFTERWARD The King smiled sourly, as the brakeman passed on. It was plain that he was very young and, for a shack, endowed with too trusting a nature. Any other brakeman would have insisted upon searching The King and then splitting the loot fifty-fifty with him, unless he chose to take the lion's share for himself.

Left to himself King Charlie took the first opportunity of going over his prize and, when he had counted it hastily, gasped with pleasure and surprise. For the one dollar bill was one of only a thin sheaf of that small denomination, and the rest of the tightly wadded money consisted of fives and tens. He counted no less than fifty tens and forty-eight fives — seven hundred and forty dollars at a single stroke — and seven hundred and forty dollars taken from no less a person than the terrible Dean himself!

The King rubbed his hands together. He felt that the warmth of youth had returned and made a springtime in his veins. To be sure it was quite probable that he had not been taking himself seriously enough of late, and that he might have wasted his time. He might return to the ways of

179

his golden period of prosperity and —

As that thought entered his mind, however, a strong shudder passed suddenly through his body. His face altered at the same moment, the jaw dropping, his cheeks falling, and the perennial color fading until his cheeks were a dusty gray. He clasped his right wrist with his left hand as strongly as he could, but in spite of that the tremor continued shaking his hands violently.

At length he cast himself back and lay flat along the top of the box car, gasping and mumbling to himself and praying that he might not start rolling toward one side, while this shuddering helplessness was upon him.

Then it passed as it had come — in a breath. He sat up slowly, weak of body, weak of soul. It was a long time since the prison tremble had seized upon him, for it was a long time since he had grossly violated the law. But now he felt as if that one long moment of agony had been sufficient payment for the entire seven hundred and forty dollars.

Later on his spirits revived, and when in the early dusk he dropped off the train at the division end, he was strong-hearted once more, for now he had in his possession the sinews of war which would enable him to go East. He could, if he wished, actually ride the cushions. But he quivered with disdain at the thought of a railroad fare passing from his hands into the hands of a railroad company! No, he would ride the rods back, since he was no longer nimble enough to ride the blind baggage. Or, better still, he would take his leisurely time and ride the slow freights, pausing at such towns as he came to, to rest and enjoy himself and going on again when he was in the mood. Until this seven hundred was spent, he would not feel the great urge to start off for unknown quarters of the world again.

Full of this resolution he stepped into a cheap restaurant near the station, while the whistle of a westbound passenger train screamed in the distance. He ordered a huge meal. Like all of his kind, King Charlie was a hearty eater when occasion served. Like the camel he could lay aboard enough solid food to last him for days. Yes, so long as there were edibles in sight, it was strange indeed if The King could not find a nook or a cranny to stow away the remnants. Now he had a long fast to make up for. His accurate nose was distinguishing, one by one, the odors which floated from the kitchen of the restaurant, and he was ordering rather by sense of smell than by the menu.

Ham and eggs, of course, started him on his course. The large platterful disappeared under his dexterous knife-and-fork work, as if by magic; it faded as a morning mist fades when the sun appears. After that he drained a great bowl of oyster stew and downed a capacious mug of coffee and hot milk. When this point had been reached he sat back in his chair and settled down to the serious study of the menu; he was now in the mood to do his real ordering of the occasion.

Just as he ordered the steak with half a dozen

eggs on top, he heard a low and strangely familiar voice saying: "Never mind that. I'll sit down over here with my friend."

And then a long, lean hand was laid upon the back of the chair opposite him. King Charlie's eyes rose slowly along the bony outlines of those fingers along and up the prodigious length of arm, which seemed an affair of bones only, under the loosely flapping sleeve of the coat, and thence up to the skinny neck and then the lean, somber face of The Dean.

King Charlie grew sick at heart and white of face, and then he smiled in answer to the terrible smile of The Dean.

"Ain't you going to ask me to sit down, pardner?" The Dean was asking.

"Why, sure," said The King. "Sit down, pal, sit down and give your order."

"Thanks," said The Dean, as he eased himself into the chair and considered the menu with a detached air, as of one to whom eating is a habit rather than a necessity, and then, having given his order, he folded his big hands on the edge of the table and regarded The King.

"A long time since I seen you, all right," he said mildly.

King Charlie studied him with a frantic interest. When The Dean was explosive he was bad enough; but when he was polite he was absolutely deadly. He drew out the wallet and pushed it across the table.

"Everything is in it except one dollar," he said.

"I met a shack that wouldn't take a dollar, and it surprised me so much that I swore on the spot that I'd give that dollar to the first person I seen when I got off the train. And the first person I seen was a dirty-faced kid. He's still hugging himself and looking at that money, I reckon."

Such an astonishing piece of news was too much for even the grim-minded Dean. He pocketed the wallet without so much as a peep at the contents.

"A shack that wouldn't take a dollar?" he asked.

"I know," said Charlie, "it don't sound reasonable, but it's a fact, son. You see, he figured that I was so old that I needed the money more'n he did. And the truth is, Dean, I ain't as young as I once was!"

Having made this plea he passed his hand over his gray head and looked appealingly at the other. But the face of The Dean was entirely disinterested.

"A gent as old as you," he said, "sure ought to figure things out before he does something that gets him into trouble. Eh?"

A cold silence ensued. At length King Charlie could stand it no longer. "You got the passenger, eh?"

"I nabbed it at the same place." A shade of wonder passed over the face of The Dean. "What's the matter with you, King? Did you think that you could get away with the stuff as easy as this? Didn't you credit me for enough brains to trail you this far? Did you think I was plumb batty?"

King Charlie shook his gray locks. "Nope. I'm

183

just getting old. I forget — old and forgetful and pretty near the end of the trail."

"Right," snapped The Dean, and his voice was as cold as winter wind. "Pretty near the end of the trail by my way of figuring!"

"Do you mean that?"

"You ornery skunk!" said The Dean. "Why, you and me had been pardners, and now you turn me down cold! You try to trim me and pass me up like a sucker."

"Dean, I didn't know you. I swear I didn't recognize you."

"Bah!"

That exclamation sealed the talk for the time being. The King looked down. Sadly he raised the knife and fork, as the vast platter with its load of steak and eggs was placed before him.

"Dean," he ventured timidly, "might you be interested in a little of this steak and egg? I've sort of lost interest in it."

Joylessly The Dean smiled. "You better eat it," he said. "I'm thinking about something that might save your rotten old hide after all. Understand? Does that give you back your appetite?"

At this King Charlie fastened upon his companion a wistful and faintly hopeful gaze, like one who knows that there is inevitable ruin ahead, and who yet hopes in spite of sure knowledge that something may be done. The sardonic face of The Dean revealed nothing. He might have been thinking of Christmas — or murder. His long fingers were clasped together on the edge of the table, and they were coiling and uncoiling ceaselessly, so that King Charlie was reminded of a spider, writhing over the body of a victim.

Suddenly the keen eyes of The Dean lifted and looked through and through him.

"Charlie!" he said.

The King choked on the morsel which he was attempting to swallow at that moment. Then he answered: "Well, Dean?"

"For what you've done, or tried to do, I sure ought to get you bad, King."

He was relenting. Such an opening sentence could mean nothing else. So The King instantly assented.

"It was sure a bad trick, Dean. I was starving — that was —"

"I know. Now, King, suppose I show you a way to pay me back. Suppose I show you how you can fix this up and make everything square, and all it will cost you is a little talk. Are you willing to talk to make this up?"

King Charlie drew a great breath. It was like receiving a pardon on the verge of execution. "I'll talk for you," he replied.

"But if you don't talk well enough," said the savage Dean, "we come right back to the starting point, is that square?"

"Yes," said The King, with a little less enthusiasm.

"The whole game is this: I was trimmed last month — I was trimmed bad!"

"You don't look it," said The King. "Not with

the front you're sporting now, son, and with that seven hundred and forty kicking around loose in your pocket!"

The Dean shook his head. "Seven hundred?" he asked with unspeakable sadness. "Seven hundred? What's that? Nothing! I'm going to tell you a story about how I had a thousand times that much in my pocket — a thousand times, King Charlie!"

CHAPTER XXIV

THE DEAN'S STORY

SEVEN hundred thousand dollars?" exclaimed The King. "You mean to say —"

"Ah, more than that," insisted The Dean with a doleful calm. "Fifty thousand more than that. Yes, sir, I had three quarters of a million in my hands, and I was done out of it by crooked work!"

At the first part of this speech, marvel and then a chilly fear for the sanity of his former friend, passed through the mind of The King. It had been close to insanity for such a man as The Dean to put a wallet in an outside overcoat pocket, for instance. But the last part of the remark changed the trend of Charlie's thoughts. Crooked work? He hardly restrained a laugh when he thought of the consummate knavery at cards by which The Dean had worked his way through the world.

"It was down in San Tone," said the melancholy Dean. "It was down in old San Tone that I met up with my good luck. It seems close onto ten years ago, but matter of fact it wasn't much more'n ten days. Down yonder I met up with my good luck. You know, Charlie, that I always used to say that I never had no fair chances, and that the reason I didn't make no progress was just because

187

I didn't meet up with the right sort of gents?"

"Many times I recollect I heard you say that," replied The King soothingly. "I sure enough remember you saying that often — all you needed was to sit down to a table where there was a million dollars, and if they was willing to play high, you'd walk away with the most part of the coin."

"Yes, I said it, and I meant it," declared The Dean proudly. "I been held down all my life by having to play with pikers, King. But all my life I was waiting for a change in the luck. Well, that change come, and one day down in San Tone I found myself sitting with four gents that could have bet at least half a million each and paid in cash the same day.

"Every one of them was playing crooked, and every one of them was as good as a professional at the cards. But I beat 'em, son. I sure trimmed 'em neat. They played me for a fall guy, but all the time I was double-crossing them, and when they thought they was leading me on, I was only plucking them proper. Big mistake which I made was that I didn't get all that I could that first day. But I thought that that was a come-on game, and that if I got 'em worked up good the first night, they'd come back the second day and I could sink the hook good and deep. So all I got away with that first evening was fifty thousand."

"Fifty thousand!" cried The King.

"Shut up, you old fool!" snarled The Dean, treading heavily on the toes of his table mate. "Don't you know that some of the boys in this place have ears and know how to use 'em?"

King Charlie murmured an apology, and The Dean went on.

"Fifty thousand was what I picked up that first day. But it looked like nothing to me. It was twenty times as much as I'd ever cleaned up before, but I was looking for enough to retire on and get respectable. I was a fool, too; for the next day those boys put their heads together and decided that I was too much for them. They all sent me notes regretting that they had business that kept them away, so that they couldn't see me in the game again. But one note was a pile different. It came from the gent that had lost the bulk of the fifty thousand to me. He'd won from the others, but he'd lost pretty heavy to me. He was along about middle age, gray-haired, hard as tacks, smooth as they make 'em. He sends me a fine little letter. He says in it that he's sorry that the game had to be broken up, and that he wishes that just he and I could get together and resume the game and play for some real stakes. It has been some time, says he in the note, since he'd sat down to a game with a gentleman who did not care how high the stakes ran, and therefore he really wished that he and I could sit down to a table at his home and play stud, because it was a better game than five-handed poker.

"When I heard that I plumped down into a chair near the window and fanned myself for a while. When I come to, and my brain began to function again, I sent him a little note telling him I'd be

189

plumb tickled to play a game with him at his house or any other house. Then I slipped downstairs in a sort of haze and asks the clerk about Judge Howick.

" 'Oh, he's worth three or four millions, any way you look at it,' says the clerk.

"I staggered away and sat down again. I seen plain that my big time had come, and that I was due for my killing and then retire and maybe found a college, or build a hospital, or something like that. I was seeing myself like that, sort of in moving pictures, with me for the hero every time, when in comes the judge himself. He gives me a wide smile and a strong hand, and ten minutes later we're on the way out to his ranch, with the dust chugging up from the hoofs of his span of high-steppers and my baggage slung into the rear of the rig.

"The judge was so agreeable he pretty near melted in the mouth all the way out. He didn't talk at all about the game of the night before, or the games to come. He was just telling me about his ranch and about how dead interested he was in raising fine cattle, and how his heart was all wrapped up in his little niece and nephew — but maybe you see how the thing works out? I hear him in a sort of a happy dream, just thanking my stars every time we go over a bump that I'd brought along every cent of that fifty thousand so that I'd have the stake and the backing I needed. And then we land at his place. Not all at once, you see, but gradual.

"We slide through about fifty thousand acres of hills and valleys and farm lands in the bottoms and grazing lands on the hills and finally we come in sight of his house. It stands on the top of a flat-headed hill, with a flock of palm trees and such like, standing around it, and the house itself just showing through here and there, one of them pink-plaster Spanish affairs, you know, with blue window trimmings. It looked nice and quiet. It didn't make no more noise than a million dollars.

"That was until you got into the inside court, the patio. That was done up for a winner. Yes, sir, you never seen the beat of that, Charlie. It had real honest-to-goodness columns all around the sides — marble columns with fool carving strung all over 'em. And there were arches in between the columns. Why, Charlie, a church couldn't have been built more plumb expensive than that house is! Everywhere I turned my head I seen a dollar sign!

"When the judge eased me out of the rig, a couple of negro boys comes running — a couple — no, there was a whole flock of 'em. One of 'em got my duster, one grabs my hat. Another couple hooks onto my suit case. Well, that was the way I managed to stagger to my little room, which was only about as big as this whole restaurant, throwing in the kitchen for luck. It had a bath off to one side and a little private garden over to the other side, with glass doors opening out onto it, and more colors in the flowers than you could name in ten minutes.

"But I'll cut out the trimmings and give you the facts about what happened in that there house — Casa Loma, they call it! We got through a fair lot of drinks that day and come down to the evening all ripe for a buster of a game, and a buster of a game it sure enough was!

"Stud is my particular pet. Maybe you know that. It hurts my feelings to take money away from the best of 'em when it comes to stud. And that night I had the pasteboards talking to me like I was their daddy. There wasn't nothing that I couldn't do to them cards, and I tied the judge into knots. He kept shaking his head and sighing and smiling, and then he'd order in another drink.

"Every time he ordered a drink, a couple of them big negroes showed up, and they sure looked like a bad time, them boys did! I never seen so much muscle roaming around loose on a couple of gents as on the two negroes that handled that liquor. Each of 'em was as big as Joe Hoyt at his palmiest."

Here King Charlie shook his head. "I reckon that's stretching it," he said.

"It ain't, I tell you," insisted The Dean. "I tell you the judge must have hand-picked the most of Africa to get two as big as them and as well matched. They had to go sidewise through the door, and when they took up a glass it looked like they couldn't help smashing it. And when one of them boys leaned over, I seen the outline of a big gat on his back pocket, printed as clear as black and white.

192

"Easy to see that they was the judge's pet bull-dogs as well as his drink-mixers. But I didn't pay no attention to them because I was blind. I noted that they jumped mighty quick whenever the judge give 'em a look, but that didn't register in my head as meaning anything in particular. I went right on playing and winning.

"Winning? You never seen so much money stacked on any one table. The judge began to sign I O Us, and pretty soon I had 'em stacked up like one dollar bills, and nearly every I O U was for a thousand or more.

"About midnight the judge allowed that it was enough for a start, and he give a sign to one of the bulldogs, and the big fellow slips an arm under the judge's shoulders and lifts him out of his chair and takes him off to put him to bed — he was that far gone with the booze.

"I took up the winnings and moseyed off to my own room, with three or four negroes to open doors for me and bow me through. When I got inside my place I made a quick dive for the lamp and shoved the pocketful of I O Us onto the table.

"Seven hundred thousand dollars was what I made out there, all wrote out in the judge's own handwriting, and all as good as gold for jury evidence if I had to go to law to collect. Well, my knees pretty near buckled under me, while I stood there looking at myself as a future regent of a university, or bank president, or something foolish like that.

"When I went to bed I lay awake for a while

and then I went to sleep and was president of a railroad all night, and I spent my time kicking hobos off of the rods. But when I woke up in the morning the thing I done was to reach my hand under my pillow. Sure enough I found my wallet there. I pulled it out and decided that I'd cast an eye over my winnings and read that signature of the judge's a dozen times by way of starting the day off right. But when I opened the wallet, there wasn't a thing in it. Only thing that I seen was a calling card. My fifty thousand was gone, and all the I O Us were gone, too.

"With a yell I hit the ceiling. Five minutes later I busted in on the judge.

" 'I been robbed!' I shouts.

" 'Impossible,' said the judge as cool as ice.

" 'Every I O U is gone,' says I.

" 'What I O Us are you referring to?' says he.

" 'Them that you signed last night,' says I.

" 'My dear fellow,' says he, 'I don't recall signing any I O Us. The liquor must have had even more effect upon you than I feared. Don't you recall having lost your cash during the game?'

"Just as I reached for my gun I felt a sort of a shadow fall over me. I turned around. One of the big black fellows was standing right behind me, with his hand dropped into his coat pocket. Sure enough he had a gun turned on me, ready to blow me to bits. In spite of himself he couldn't hold back a grin that split his face right in half.

"I turned around to the judge, and he said:

'Now, my friend, I hope your reason and memory have been restored.'

"Well, I seen that it was no use. If I tried to make a kick, he could have me locked up. His negroes would swear any sort of evidence against me. Besides my record wouldn't look none too good if they started prying into my past.

" 'Judge,' says I, 'I see that it needs a training on the bench to keep a man's head clear while he's drinking.'

" 'Ah,' says he, smiling as cool as you please, 'my title is purely honorary, thank you!'

"And that morning one of the negroes drove me back to town. And that's the reason, King, that seven hundred don't mean nothing in my life. You understand? Nothing means nothing to me until I get a chance to come back at him! And that's why I've told you this story — because you got the means to help me out!"

CHAPTER XXV

THE DEAN DEALS

ONCE again King Charlie looked somberly upon his company as if suspicious of the sanity of The Dean. Then he said: "Look here, pal, I know you got me backed into a corner, and you got a right to ask anything I can do. But all that you and me and ten like us could do wouldn't budge the judge. Howick seems to be one of them gents that can pull a crooked deal now and then, but who have the country behind 'em, and —"

"Behind him? I should say not! The record of Howick is just short of good enough to land him in prison. He's worked up from nothing, and he worked up by grub-staking prospectors and then beating them out of their half of the claims when they landed something worth while. He's the best hated man in Texas, and you can lay to that! If he was to go down, the police would sure weep if they had to arrest them that stung him. Old Howick knows it, and that's why he's got his place full of those man-killing negroes. They'd as soon wring a gent's neck as look at him, and that's why the judge has them out there. He knows that he has to fight his own battles, and he keeps a standing army of his own to do it! But when I got to thinking things over I seen that I knew only two men that could help me. One was Joe Hoyt, because Joe is the only man I know strong enough to handle one of those big black fellows. And the other, King, is a man that nobody but you can get to go with me, and he's the only man that I know of in the whole world that's smart enough and dangerous enough to tackle Judge Howick. That's Billy English!"

King Charlie pushed his plate back and shook his head.

"If you want to get even because I lifted that wallet," he said, "take me out and fill me full of lead, but don't ask me to try to lead Billy English crooked. Besides, I couldn't do it!"

"You couldn't? Ain't you his father?"

With a sigh King Charlie dropped his head. How often would that tremendous lie he had told rise again to haunt him? With that lie he had forced an honest youngster to go wrong. In spite of that lie Billy English had torn himself away from the life of the long riders and had chosen honest work.

"Dean," he said, "you don't understand. It's ten years since Billy has seen me. I've seen him, but it was only by sneaking close and peeking in, you might say, every couple of years. The rest of the time I've spent back around New York, where I'm to home. But every couple of years I've sneaked out and taken a look at Billy and the girl."

"The girl?" asked The Dean. "I didn't know that he was interested in any skirt."

"You forget. I mean the little five-year-old kid

that him and Joe Hoyt and me and you, Dean, swore that we'd try to help after her mother died in that lodging house —"

"Louise Alison Dora Young — I remember," cried The Dean suddenly. "Lady!"

"Lady," replied The King gravely. "That's what we called her. But what one of us has kept his word by her? Only Billy. He cut out the crooked work, and he went straight for the sake of that kid. He was only sixteen when he started slaving to make a home for that little youngster. He's twenty-six now. He started in with nothing. I've seen him four times, and every time he'd done something more. Right now he has a nice little herd of cows started. All of the folks in that part of the country swear by him. Lady has growed into a fine-looking kid. I seen her two years back, kind of long in the legs and wabbly in the knees, but a disposition like a day in May and a smile like a bird singing. She —"

"Look here, Charlie," asked The Dean grimly, "are you writing a book about Lady, or are you telling me whether or not you'll get Billy English to help me out? I know that he's gone straight. That's just because he's a fool. Why, when he started he was only a kid — only fifteen — but inside of a year he had the makings of the best yegg I ever seen. He could read the mind of the tumblers, and he could make his guns talk Latin for him. He went straight. Now I'm going to do him a good turn and show how, by making one more crooked turn and taking one more long ride,

198

he can make enough to set up a real home. Understand? Howick is so hated, and he hates everybody else so much, that he won't do business with banks. He keeps his cash in his own safe, and he has his own safe guarded, all with his own men. Charlie, listen!"

He laid a hand of iron upon the wrist of the older man and leaned across the table.

"There's at least a cool quarter of a million in that safe of his. Understand? A share to you and another to Hoyt. Two shares apiece for Billy English and me. Is that square. Forty thousand for you, King?"

King Charlie leaned back in his chair, his mind distraught with anguish. In him there was an honest desire to play fair, to keep from tempting the youth who believed that he was the son of the tramp, King Charlie. But it was only a few moments before that he had had in his hands the seven hundred and forty, and the thought of fifty times that sum dazzled him.

Like all of the criminal class, a crime proposed was to him a crime accomplished; the mention of a quarter of a million established exactly that sum as the prize, and it established it so clearly that he could almost see the denominations of the bills in the drawers of the safe.

So he wavered, fighting the battle back and forth until he heard the insidious whisper of the other: "Remember, Charlie, if you can't do this for me, there's another way out, and that's for you and me to meet outside and —"

King Charlie nodded. "You've got me, Dean," he said. "I'll do what I can. But how do we get to Billy's place?"

"We start in the morning. Meet me here."

Without another word The Dean rose and left the place. After he was gone, leaving his untouched food behind him, but tossing The King a bill which would pay for the meal and buy a bed for the night, the old tramp drank another cup of coffee and pondered. His first thought, of course, was to flee, but he knew well enough that, without money, his course along the rails would be much slower than that of The Dean. He could not hope to distance the younger and more active man, and the end of the chase was sure to end in a killing, when The Dean took vengeance for this second act of treachery.

He was being played on a long rope, but he could only use it to hang himself. So he paid the bill, left the restaurant, and found a bed.

In the morning he rose early and went straight back to the restaurant where, as he half expected, he found the lean form of The Dean waiting for him. The latter allowed him only time to make the briefest of breakfasts, and then, when a train whistled, bound west, tore him from his chair and started him toward the track.

It was a lumbering freight, heavily loaded. They took the rods side by side, and during the day The Dean impressed upon The King again and again the undying hatred which he felt for Judge Howick. It was not only that he had been basely tricked, he told his traveling mate, but it was because Howick had violated the code of honor among thieves. A crook himself, he yet sheltered himself behind the standard and the position of an honest man.

Until late afternoon they stayed with that train, then they dropped off and took a branch line, riding the cushions into a cattle country. At the end of the line they climbed down and found themselves in a typical little cow town.

"Here's where we ought to find Joe Hoyt," said The Dean. "I've kept track of him the past ten years. He's spent seven of 'em breaking rock, so he ought to be in good trim. He's only out for the last six months, matter of fact."

"Then he'll be sore-headed and mean as a grizzly," said The King.

Very much like a grizzly was his appearance, at least, when they came upon him. They found him readily upon inquiry. His name was changed, of course, but his description was unmistakable, and they found him seated upon the veranda of the hotel, gazing toward the western hills, where a long line of cattle ambled against the red of the sunset sky.

He was a vast-shouldered man, without much claim to a neck, but with a huge head growing directly out of his chest. His arms were of great length, and when he stood up they arched out pronouncedly from his sides, because of the swelling muscles. His hair was a gray mane, as coarse as the mane of a horse and quite long, so that when he removed his sombrero it was apt to fall in a ragged shower low on his forehead.

Upon The King and The Dean he turned the lackluster eye of one who did not at all recollect them, and The Dean smiled upon his companion.

"He's still got some wits left under that thick skull of his!" he said. "I'll open up the talk." Stepping close to Joe Hoyt, he said: "Well, stranger, appears like you was thinking pretty hard just now. Are we intruding if we ask you a few questions?"

"Talk," said Joe Hoyt, "is tolerable cheap. Talk don't bother me none. So blaze away and tell me what's what. Are you new to these parts?"

"Plumb new. What do they raise around here?"

"Trouble," said Joe Hoyt without lifting his voice. "Mostly they raise trouble."

"Maybe you're a farmer yourself in that class," suggested The King.

"Yes, I raise greenbacks," said Joe Hoyt with perfect seriousness. "That's the crop that I hope to harvest, bo."

"Have you got it sowed?"

"Run out of seed," said Joe Hoyt.

Then he glanced over his shoulder and made out that they were in no immediate danger of interruption.

"What's the game?" he asked. "And how in hell are you?"

"Flush," said The Dean, "and a fine plant all worked up — one that we need you in on."

"I been sitting here waiting and waiting and waiting," Hoyt said. "I've been waiting for something to happen, and now luck has turned my way! Dean, when do we eat!"

"You see," said The Dean, chuckling, "he ain't lost his old tricks. He's still strong on the eats. Have you got your grip yet, Joe?"

Joe Hoyt leaned over close to the chair in which The Dean had seated himself. He slipped his hand under the seat of the chair and without rising, without showing the slightest strain, he lifted the chair and The Dean in it and brought him nearer.

"Sit nearer," said Joe Hoyt. "My hearing ain't up to what it used to be."

The Dean nodded. "Ten years," he said, "ain't changed your muscles any, pardner. Now listen to me!"

CHAPTER XXVI

FOR LADY

IT was twenty-four hours later. Crouched outside the window, Joe Hoyt and The King and The Dean were looking into the interior of the house. What they saw was the simplest sort of a rancher's cabin. There was only one room below. The stove, both for cooking and for heating, was in one corner. The homemade table was in the center, with the ax marks visible on the legs which supported it. The chairs were of almost equally crude manufacture. The floor was of the rudest planks, with the skin of a puma here and the skin of a bear there, to soften the boards, skins so badly mutilated that they would have brought no price as pelts in the market. A saddle hung by the stirrup in a corner. A bridle was draped on the horn. Revolver and gun belt were hooked across the top of a rifle which leaned against the wall. A ladder to one side showed the way to the trap above, which opened the entrance to the sleeping quarters.

But the center of interest on which the three observers focused their attention was that circle of lamplight around the table, where sat Billy English, tilted back in his chair and smoking a cig-

204

arette, with the enjoyment which only comes at the end of a long day's work. He looked all of his twenty-six years, and more than all of them. He had taken the burden of a man's responsibilities at a period when most men are still without a serious thought. And, with ten years of constant and heavy labor behind him, his lean young face was seamed and saddened by worry. Yet his blue eye was bright and intense and restless in its rovings, though it now fixed steadily upon the girl at the opposite end of the table.

Her back was toward the window. They could see chiefly the rounded nape of her neck and the heavy braid of yellow hair which slipped down past her shoulders and stirred in all its shimmering length whenever she moved her head. She moved it often, looking up from the book which she was reading aloud to him.

As she read, now and again a slender brown hand flew out in an expressive gesture, or her head would turn a little in the excess of her emotion, and the watchers caught sight of a white, gleaming forehead, where hats had sheltered her from the sun, and the pleasant profile of a girl of fifteen.

Her auditor, at least, seemed to find more of interest in her face than in her words. He had not that intent look which comes to a listener of the spoken word, but he pored intently upon her face, as if it carried a heart-filling message to him, the same thing over and over and never wearying.

"That's her," said King Charlie, "and that's him. Would you ever have knowed 'em?"

"Never would have knowed either of 'em," said Joe Hoyt.

"Would have knowed both of 'em if you hadn't been within a thousand miles of me when I seen 'em," said The Dean. "I can tell the girl by her looks. I can tell Billy English by that look in his eye, as if he had just finished fighting somebody, or else was just about to fight somebody. Never seen so much bull terrier in any man's face as there is in his!"

Presently they knocked at the door, and it was opened to them by Lady. At the first dim sight of three men in the night, she smiled instinctively. Plainly she had been taught to trust all men. It was only when she caught sight of the lowering face and the tremendous bulk of Joe Hoyt that she gave back a startled half step.

As she turned, the lamplight gleamed a ruddy gold along her hair and outlined all of her features with a glow. Of one accord the three men in the outer night caught their breath. It was not her beauty of the moment so much as the promise of her beauty to come, and above all a brave-eyed, clean-lipped girlishness which went to their hearts. She had turned a little toward Billy English as she stepped back.

The latter came out of his seat like a panther which sleeps coiled up one instant and the next is leaping at the throat of that which awakens it. So he came toward the door, a meager form, not above the average in height or bulk and small compared with the lofty height of The Dean or the

206

burly form of Joe Hoyt. Yet Billy English was large enough. He made up by the perfect balance of eye and hand, the speed of movement, the symmetrical proportions which would enable him to put forth surprising efforts, for his lack of sheer weight of bone and muscle.

As he peered into the night he exclaimed, and then strode out and caught King Charlie by both shoulders.

"I've been waiting, and here you are." Then he turned on the others. His first enthusiasm suddenly waned. His greeting was icy cold. "How are you, Dean? How are you, Hoyt? Come in!"

They accepted the invitation, all silent, because he had not offered to shake hands with any except The King.

"Lady," he said, turning to the girl, "I want you to know some folks I used to be acquainted with. This is Charlie — King, this is Mr. — Dean, and this is Mr. — Josephs."

He hesitated each time a little as he turned their sobriquets into proper names.

"This is Louise Young," he said to the men, and she went from one to the other around the little semicircle and shook hands with them. "Run upstairs," he added to her. "I got to talk business to these old — friends of mine."

Only for an instant the girl paused, but in that interval she fixed upon the trio, each in turn, a glance of terror and the utmost penetration. Then she went obediently up the ladder and disappeared. No sooner was she gone than the attitude of Billy

English changed, and his smile went out.

"Now," he murmured sternly, "talk soft. She guesses that something is wrong, and she has the ear of a deer. What are you fellows up to?"

Putting King Charlie out of the conversation, so to speak, by turning a shoulder upon him, in the meantime he fixed the other two with a cold eye. "Talk out," he said. "You two never traveled together before for any good, and I'm surprised if you're traveling together now for the sake of your health. What is it you want?"

Joe Hoyt was beginning to bridle under this stinging stream of sarcasm, but The Dean interposed with soft words.

"First of all," he said, "I want to know why you're so hard on us, Billy? We used to be pals once. Why are you so hard on us now? We ain't going to steal the girl away from you, Billy!"

"You've left her in the lurch for ten years," said Billy fiercely. "You left her for a kid, like I was ten years ago, to take care of. How in the name of Heaven I was able to pull her through the first couple of winters I dunno, what with her sick most of the time and me part of the time. But if I managed, it wasn't no credit to you, none of you! You swore you'd stand by her and help her out. And here's the first time in ten years that you've showed up!"

The Dean raised his hand to protest against the torrent of angry words.

"It's easy to talk without really knowing," he declared. "But just wait until you know a few of the facts, son. Here is Joe has been in the pen for six years. Here's me that has run in such rotten luck that I've hardly been able to take care of myself, let alone helping to take care of anybody else. But the minute I got a chance to help I come. It took ten years for that chance to show up. But when it came I started for you."

"Because you need me," said Billy, "and because you hope you can work me in on one of your crooked games, but I'm through with all that. I'm clean through!"

For the moment The Dean was a little taken aback because his motives had been so readily deciphered. But he gathered himself together as well as he could and confronted Billy English again.

"You're hot under the collar now, Billy," he said, "but you'll get over that. Wait till your father has had a chance to talk to you."

Billy English turned like a flash upon King Charlie and, with a strange mixture of pity and horror, of sadness and hatred, stared at the old tramp, who now had mustered his bravest air as he clasped Billy upon the shoulder and said: "You mustn't go off half-cocked like this. You got to give people a chance to explain themselves. If you won't listen to The Dean, just listen to me!"

The other shrank from under the extended hand. The Dean called Joe Hoyt away with a gesture, and they went toward the stove to make a pretense of warming their hands, while their orator strove to convince Billy.

Short and vigorous was the argument which he advanced.

"How long you been living here, Billy?"

"You know as well as I do — ten years."

"How many days of work have you missed in that time?"

"I dunno. Maybe three or four weeks when I was sick."

"Cold and hot, wet and dry, you have been out in all sorts of weather, riding the range. I can see it in your face, Billy. You look all wore out!"

"Yes, what of it?"

"What of it? Why just this: What have you got out of it? Where are you now ahead of where you were ten years ago?"

"Ten years ago Lady was a baby five years old. I've give her ten years of an honest life. She's got her schooling in them ten years, and she's lived happy!"

"Is that what you've got ahead?" asked The King. It was more than he had expected, and he was fighting for a moment of time. "Is that all?"

"Ain't that enough?" asked Billy. "I can get along without being rich. Besides, I got some cows. Every year the herd grows. I like the business, and I get along fine with the folks in these parts. I ain't got much in the way of dollars to show for my work, but I got some results. Maybe before I die I'll have the dollars, too. I'm not worrying about that. The main thing is that Lady has had a chance —"

"To live like a lady?" asked The King.

"A lady? What d'you mean? If being honest and around honest folks and growing up polite and kind-hearted — if that makes a lady, then she is one!"

"But you and me both know that that ain't the only thing. Remember the way her mother talked? Remember the way her mother had her dressed? Billy, she was meant to be raised like a lady of leisure, and you know it. And out here, what are you raising her up to be? The drudge on some ranch — that's all! What sort of advantages have you got to show her?"

Billy English dropped his head.

"What school is she going to now? She's gone through grammar school. Where's the high school to send her to? But, better still, she'd ought to go to a finishing school where she could learn manners and get the ways of a lady as well as the name of one!"

"I never thought about them things — not in that way," muttered the younger man. "Maybe you're right, but how am I to do all that?"

"That," said King Charlie, breathing a sigh of relief as he neared victory, "is what I've come to tell you about. I ain't suggesting that you do anything for your own sake, but just for the sake of the girl."

As Billy English started to speak he changed his mind and dropped into a chair. From the corner by the stove The Dean waved his arms in sign of victory and urged King Charlie on.

211

CHAPTER XXVII

LA CASA LOMA

RISING from his chair Judge Howick made a signal. Instantly a giant negro stepped from the shadow of the patio arcade and drew back the chair. When the judge resumed his seat he was turned half toward the sun and half away from it, for the sunlight was now a brilliant red gold, having reached that low point in the west when the white heat which it carried all day began to be lost and filtered away through the screen of atmosphere before it reached the earth. The judge stretched himself into a new position of comfort and regarded the angle which the shadow of the opposite roof made on the side of the arcade. It had been rapidly sloping athwart the floor of the patio, and now it was climbing the columns, inch by inch.

"It's time for them to be here," he said aloud. "I've told that fool Murphy to make faster time between the house and the station. Eh, Jules?"

Jules, the big negro, who had just moved the chair and now attended the master silently, stepped forward again to answer.

"He says it kills the horses when they make the drive in an hour, sir," he said. "He aims to make it a little less because —"

"Curse his reasons and curse him!" exploded Howick. "I told him to make the trip in exactly one hour. If he uses up a few horses, that makes no difference. What in thunder is a horse or two, here or there? If I can afford to spend horses in order to make fast time, who's to say no to me, eh? Who's to stop me, Jules?"

This last was delivered in a roar, and big Jules spread out his hands in a gesture of resignation. The judge now jerked out his watch and stared at it.

"He's got three minutes left," he said, "and —"

Gloomy disappointment took the place of the savage look as he heard the crunching of the hoofs far off on the road. It seemed that he would have treasured the opportunity to fall upon poor Murphy. But now the buckboard came to a halt in front of the patio, and there appeared two down-headed grays, dripping sweat and flecked with the white foam of their labors.

Murphy himself, an active little man, with an expression of black rage now on his face, appeared, conducting another and taller fellow. As they came up, Howick waved the one to a chair and turned inquiringly upon Murphy.

"Look!" cried the latter in a choked voice. "Look at them hosses! The near mare is half killed, and the off ain't much better. Neither of 'em'll be good for a lick of work for a week!"

"Then don't work them for a week — or work them to death, curse them, and buy a horse that can stand the trip!"

"No hosses ain't born that can stand that trip regular. If they can make the trip in, they can't stand the trip back on the same day. It'd kill the best that ever walked. Maud S. couldn't make that double trip and stand up under it!"

"Let the worries of the stable stay in the stable," said Howick sternly. "This is the patio of my house."

Murphy exploded with a shout of horror and rage. "Because you pay money for your hosses, d'you think you got a right to *murder* 'em?"

Howick raised his hand and pointed. "Get out," he said, "and don't come back until you're ready with an apology!"

Murphy hesitated, trembling with fury, and then turned and fairly ran from the patio. The man whom he had brought into the inclosure, now gingerly took his chair, still with his head turned to watch the place where Murphy had disappeared.

"That fellow will do you harm one of these days," he said. "He means no good to you, Mr. Howick!"

"None of 'em do," replied the latter quietly.

"There's hardly a man on my place that wouldn't knife me if I turned my back on him. That's a fact, Johnson."

Young Johnson regarded his host with more critical interest than surprise.

"I'd rather tame lions," he said. "I'd rather lie down among man-eaters than stay around men I know hate me. That fellow Murphy, now — his

214

face sticks in my memory. I seemed to remember having seen him somewhere and —"

"Stop worrying about that. Of course you've seen him. He's Jack Murphy, and you've seen his picture in the rogues' gallery. He has two killings to his credit, but they were never able to hang much on him — never enough to send him up for it. I got hold of him. He has one weakness. He loves horses. So I find him useful. Also he amuses me!"

"Because it drives him nearly crazy to have to drive his horses at the rate you demand?" asked Johnson, with a slight sneer.

"You ask too many questions!" replied Howick. "Suppose I were to send some one to ask as many questions of you?"

Johnson changed color. "To get down to the business of my report," he said in a brusque and matter-of-fact manner.

"Go ahead with it then. Have you been watching him as far as this? How far East did he go?"

"East? He didn't go East."

"Not East? You don't mean to say that a gambler of his talent is wasting his time in the West?"

"That's just what I mean. He's gone West with his grievance."

"Grievance?"

"I mean what he calls a grievance. He persists in saying that he was robbed of fifty thousand dollars in your house, together with an enormous number of I O Us which you had signed."

"A peculiar illusion," said Howick and smiled

mirthlessly. "But go on with your story. Instead of going East he went West to play in some of the small towns until he had secured a stake again?"

"He hasn't been gambling lately," said Johnson. "He has been gathering men instead of dollars. Three men, Mr. Howick."

"What the devil does he mean by that?"

"He means trouble for you, sir."

"Trouble for me?" Judge Howick broke into uproarious laughter. Then he rose, paced up and down a few times in the keenness of his delight at the thought, and then planted himself in his chair again. "This promises to be a good game," he went on. "He's got together three men, and the four of them are going to give me trouble, eh?"

"I wouldn't smile," said Johnson. "I'd take it a little seriously."

"Perhaps you would. That's because you haven't been through what I've been through. I know these things, Johnson. I love peril. A touch of danger is the sauce that makes existence worth while. But why in the name of Heaven do you think that I, surrounded by men who would die for me simply because they know that they would soon die without me — guarded by such men as these, why under Heaven, Johnson, should I fear four lone men? Who are they?"

"One is an old tramp, well over sixty, and afflicted with the prison trembles or shakes as they call it. That's a sort of nervous ague, you know."

"Certainly a formidable start," observed Howick with a grin. "Who are the others?"

"The other is a gigantic fellow named Hoyt, just out of prison after serving a six-year term and ready for any sort of deviltry. He has a long record behind him."

"If the law has been clever enough to catch him so many times, do you think that I shall have any trouble with him? This Dean man isn't as clever as I thought. Has he lost his mind that he thinks of tackling me with such a picked-up aggregation of loafers and ex-convicts? Who's the third man?"

"A youngster twenty-six years old."

"No man under thirty is dangerous," said Howick instantly. "They may possess both skill and courage, but without mellowing experience they are not dangerous. What's his record?"

"For ten years he has ridden range."

"Dean *is* mad!"

"I think not. I have made inquiries about the gang of them. Nothing was very definitely known. But there is a pretty general rumor, according to a man I met from Colorado, that Billy English once operated with Hoyt and The Dean, and they made a terrible trio. Dean was the schemer, Hoyt was the bulldog and the muscle of the party, and Billy English — he was only a kid of fifteen or sixteen then — was the fighting edge of the instrument. It was a good enough tool to cut through pretty strong safes, Mr. Howick."

"Ah, you think they contemplate burglary — burglary of my safe?"

"Not an unreasonable surmise," said Johnson coldly.

"Where are they now?"

"Here."

"What?"

"I mean it. They must be somewhere among the hills near the house. I suppose right now they're boiling down the powder to make the soup."

The nearness of the danger sobered even the confident Howick. Then he shrugged his shoulders.

"But the point is," he said, "that they don't understand my system of guarding the safe. Do you understand it, Johnson?"

"No."

"Suppose you take a turn down in the cellar with me. You'll be amused."

Passing down a wide and easy flight of stairs which opened onto the patio arcade, they reached the series of capacious rooms which formed the cellars of La Casa Loma. For, since the weather during most of the year was bitingly hot, far more of La Casa was an excavation in the living rock than showed above the ground. There were two, and even three, levels of lofty rooms.

"It's been a fancy and a hobby with me," the owner explained. "Digging these rooms has made me feel like the proprietor of a genuine donjon."

They spent a full hour wandering through the lower regions of the house and examining the workings of the defenses of the safe. When they came up again Johnson was white and sick of face.

"Well," said Howick cheerfully, "confess that you have never seen defenses like that around a safe."

"Never," said Johnson, "have I seen a safe surrounded with such traps. The safe, it seems, is only the bait!"

CHAPTER XXVIII

THE CAPTIVE

THE resolution of Howick was that he would remain on the alert during every instant of the evening. But there is nothing so fatiguing as the constant expectation of danger which is delayed over even the shortest interval. Before ten in the evening the judge, as he was called for no known reason, began to yawn and stretch his thick, strong arms. Finally he turned and asked Johnson how he could manage to keep awake so long and so easily.

"It's because you don't give a hang what happens to me," he complained. "There's no strain on you, Johnson."

"None at all," said Johnson. "If you think a moment, you'll see that it's better this way. You've hired me as a combination bloodhound and bulldog; you'd better keep me in that capacity. If I begin to worry I'll be less efficient."

Howick glowered at his private detective. Like all of the other men in his employ, he knew that he could trust Johnson simply because he had enough on the detective to send him to prison. But, though he ruled all of his people by fear and money, there were times when he realized that

220

there is something more important than that which can be bought for cash.

"Your heart isn't in your work, Johnson," he said. "I know that."

"Of course not," admitted Johnson frankly. "That isn't the point, is it?"

Judge Howick favored him with another vicious look and then yawned again.

"Well, I'm going to bed," he announced at last. "How are the men posted?"

"Just as you ordered them to be posted," said Johnson. "I had them all in their places before dark."

Instinctively he looked up as he spoke. The patio was a pool of black, shot across here and there with an uncertain glow from hanging lamps under the arcade. It required some concentration to make out the dim twinkling of the stars. In the center of the patio, since the night was coming on unexpectedly hot for this season of the year, the fountain had been set to playing, and its crisp whispering ran up and down a soft scale, as the wind dipped into the inclosure and shook the head of the column of spray.

"Certainly," said Howick with another frown, "it's a foolish thing to be besieged like this — a whole fortress by four rats!"

"A rat," said Johnson coldly, "can sink the biggest ship in the world, if the ship is made of wood. Four such rats as these could gnaw even through the walls of a fortress, I should think."

"Do you mean that?" asked Howick in alarm.

221

"Nonsense!" said Johnson. "What can they do? We have about twenty trained fighters, haven't we? I've scattered half a dozen around on the high points near the house. It will take careful work to get through that line of outposts. But if they come closer, they will be met by a dozen excellent riflemen scattered around the house and instructed to shoot to kill. But even supposing that they were to penetrate through these and come to the core of affairs — the safe itself — why, Mr. Howick, don't you think that that trap would be strong enough to take them all and keep them for you?" Johnson blinked and shivered a little as he made this suggestion.

"Yes," declared Howick, "I have a good deal of faith in that trap. The point is, Johnson, that I have no reason to fear anything, and yet, when I recall the evil face of that gambler when I last saw him, I'm ready to expect well-nigh anything from him. Still, they can't work by mystery and get —"

Suddenly both he and Johnson were brought out of their chairs by a shout which was almost a shriek, not twenty paces from the gate of the patio, and at the same time their ears were struck by the sharp and ringing report of a rifle.

From the shadowy arcade the two monster negro guards, Jules and his brother, sprang to the center of the patio. They had taken off their coats and their shoes and socks. They were dressed in skin-tight, sleeveless shirts. Their huge bare feet gripped the stones of the patio pavement. The

222

muscles of their great arms bulged and slipped at each movement. For all their bulk they were as agile as two huge cats. One carried a crooked knife, with a point so keen that the blade seemed to taper off to a ray of light. The other bore a long revolver. His knife remained in his belt.

But that first leap forward had been a blind one, the result of long training that, no matter what happened, they must first protect the life of the master. Afterward they sprang to the side again and toward the gate of the patio and crouched there in tigerish silence, ready to spring upon and rend the first assailant to enter.

Howick, white with excitement, looked with a flash of profound pleasure upon these trained man-killers. Then, his gun in his hand, he awaited developments.

They were not long in coming. There was a stir and then two of Howick's men came through the entrance, half carrying and half shoving before them, as a prisoner, a tall, rosy-faced old fellow whose hat had fallen off, exposing a gray head.

"It's King Charlie," said the private detective. "It's the old tramp himself. Has the old fool gone mad and made a forlorn attack on us?"

Now the prisoner was brought to a halt before the little table at which the rancher and the detective were standing. Presently they sat down again.

"Jules!" called Howick.

Moving as silently as a cloud shadow that slips

223

across the hills, the huge negro was instantly before them.

"You boys can go back," said the rancher. "First tell me how you got him."

A scar-faced fellow stepped half a stride forward, as if taking upon himself the duties of a spokesman.

"I was lying out on the hill," he said, "when I thought that I seen something moving down in the hollow. I give Dick, here, a rap in the ribs and whispered to him to look. He seen it, too. We thought that the four was about to try a rush from that direction, but we thought that we'd wait and see a bit more before we turned in an' reported. And pretty soon Dick, who's got uncommon good eyes, made out that there was only one. We waited till he got close.

"Then I shoved a slug right over his head. He jumped and held up his hands. 'I surrender, boys,' says he. And here he is, sir!"

"Very neat work," said Howick. "I'll remember you for it. Now get back to your post. There are three more, and when they show up they may not be as easy as this one."

As they turned away, big Jules sidled forward until King Charlie was forced to look into his grinning, wicked face. Then he returned to his post behind the prisoner.

"Now," said Howick, "what are *you* doing around at this hour of the night?"

"Me?" asked King Charlie. "Why, I was just taking a stroll and waiting for the moon to come up. When I seen your house I thought it looked big enough to give me a hand-out, so I started for it. On the way a gun goes off in front of me. I jumped up —"

"You jumped up? You were crawling up the hill, then?"

King Charlie became suddenly silent.

"Well, I ain't much of a talker," he declared. "I've said my piece. That's all you get out of me!"

Howick glanced aside at the detective.

"I think what he knows might be worth extracting, don't you, Johnson?"

Johnson frowned and then, as understanding came to him, changed color: "That's up to you to decide. For my part nobody knows *anything* that's worth a price as big as that. But you're the doctor."

"You're too squeamish, Johnson," said the rancher. "That's what keeps you back in the world. You have too many nerves. You let them get in your way. Much better to take my attitude. Keep your nerves in their right place — out of sight. Jules, bring Charlie along after us to my room."

With Johnson at his side Howick led the way into the house and to a big room in the end of one of the wings. Here the owner of La Casa Loma had outdone himself. The click of their heels was lost in a soft, thick carpet. Old Italian furniture glimmered in dull polish under the lamplight. Howick threw himself into the depths of a big chair, pointed Johnson to another, and then ordered Jules to strip the shirt from the back of his prisoner, first tying both his hands and feet.

Jules replied with a grin which showed the glint of white teeth and laid a hand on King Charlie, but the latter had fallen into a violent trembling. At sight of this Johnson leaned forward with a curious look.

"That's the penitentiary shake," he said. "The King must be an old-timer. Mr. Howick, I think he'll talk now if he can, in spite of his chattering teeth."

"Will you tell us what you know?" asked Howick. "Or do you want a taste of a persuader?"

King Charlie rested a shoulder against the wall and slumped close to it. He seemed on the verge of a collapse.

"I'll talk," he said. "Heaven knows I want to stay straight with the boys, but — I couldn't stand it!"

"You show good sense," said Howick, though there was a shade of disappointment in his eye.

"Now, King Charlie, if that's what you're called, tell us what your companions are up to?"

"From this side, I was to make the feint," said King Charlie. "I was to come right up toward the patio and get myself caught. But the other three, after the noise on this side, were to tackle the house from the far side."

An exclamation broke from the rancher. "That's nerve for you, Johnson! He throws himself into the fire! Do you know that this means a fat prison term?"

"Oh, I'm used to that," answered The King

heavily. "That wouldn't stop me. Besides we expected to make enough to make it worth while. But we didn't look for you to try torture. We knew you were hard, but not this hard!"

"Ah," murmured Howick, "you see that I fool them, Johnson, in exactly the same manner that I fool you. Jules, tell your brother what I've heard. Let him go to the boys and tell them to gather and watch the far side of the house. They needn't mind about this. Then come back and stand at the door. Hurry!"

Jules was gone at once, and Howick settled back again.

"Go through The King, Johnson, will you?" he asked. "See what weapons he carries."

"He's been searched already," said Johnson, "and they've done a good job."

"Then untie the ropes and let him sit down. You can put that pair of handcuffs on him, if you will. Ah, now we're fixed for a comfortable little chat."

Lighting a cigarette he regarded the shivering and down-headed victim with mingled scorn and cruel pleasure.

"Just how much," he asked, "did the four of you expect to take out of the safe?"

"Fifty thousand," said The King heavily.

"Only that much? Ah, I see why you have failed. Lack of imagination, inability to see the truth, simply because the truth is bigger than you are." Here he turned to Johnson. "My friend, if I were to go in for this work I think

227

I could make a success of it."

"No doubt about it," said Johnson. "You have the nerve for it and mind for it!"

Howick regarded him closely to make out the truth about this rather dubious compliment, and in the meantime there was a whisper of naked feet along the flagged passage outside the door. Jules, having accomplished his mission, had returned. A moment later there was a shot and then a volley on the far side of the house.

"They're at it!" cried Howick. "The fools have run right into my trap. Johnson, I'm more and more pleased with myself. I begin to think that most of my talents are wasted in this peaceful life!"

Here, King Charlie, looking toward the door and fascinated by the glowing eyes and gleaming teeth of Jules in the dark outside, saw that worthy's head suddenly jerk back, and the next instant his whole body was jerked out of sight and fell with a heavy thud.

CHAPTER XXIX

ENTER BILLY ENGLISH

WHAT the devil is that?" asked Howick. The explosion of rifles had not been repeated. Now there was complete silence over the house. "What happened to Jules at the door? Jules!" called the judge.

"He stumbled, and then he went down the hall," said King Charlie.

"Stumbled — went down the hall? What in thunder does he mean by leaving the door when I've told him to stay there? I'll have every inch of his black hide torn from his body if he —"

Springing from his chair and hurrying to the door, he converted his fury from words into action.

"Jules!" he called loudly, and then he stepped out of sight into the hall.

Silence resulted.

King Charlie leaned back in his chair and yawned. But Johnson, the private detective, leaned forward and watched the old tramp with keen eyes.

"You old devil!" he said suddenly. "You've been covering something up. That yawn is too elaborate to suit me. You ought to be thinking of a ten-year stretch instead of sleep. What's the truth about Howick?"

He broke off his questioning to call cautiously

229

after the judge, but there was no response, and then he stepped out toward the door. "Howick!" he called a little louder and drew his revolver.

Before he could level it, however, a masked man stepped swiftly and noiselessly into the doorway and covered him with a weapon held as steady as a rock.

"Now watch that gun hand of yours, stranger," said the newcomer in a soft, almost purring voice. "Be careful that you move slow when you put that gun on the table over yonder. If you make any sudden starts, I'm going to drill you. Move lively, but let your hand work slow."

There was something so businesslike in this command that Johnson, without an attempt at resistance, backed to the table under the window, deposited his gun on it, and then shoved his hands above his head. The masked man, in spite of his haste, had time to remark scornfully:

"Look at that! They were too much rushed to take the key out — the blockheads!"

He twisted the key of the handcuffs, and King Charlie rose from the chair a free man and slipped them over the wrists of Johnson.

"I sure hate to see this happen," he assured Johnson with a grin. "But you were starting in to ask me embarrassing questions, stranger. If you keep your mouth shut, no harm'll come to you. I remember that you weren't for putting the screws to me to make me talk. I'll keep that in your favor, Johnson!"

Johnson, securely handcuffed, was pushed back

into a chair. The King then hurried to the door with his rescuer.

"You never worked better in your life, Billy," he said to his companion, as they entered the hall. "You never done a neater or a smoother job — never! Don't seem like you could have been away from the game for ten years!"

"Shut up," said Billy English sternly. "We got no time for chatter. Help me get these back into the room!"

On the floor of the flagged hall King Charlie saw the cause for the disappearance of the huge negro and the judge. The negro lay on the floor, with his mighty arms cast out; the judge was huddled in a heap.

"Are they dead — did you kill 'em both?" asked King Charlie.

"You blockhead — I never kill. There ain't a game in the world that's worth that price. Chloroform over the face and a knee in a small of the back fixed the black one. Don't you smell it still? He won't be kicking for half an hour, and we'll be out of here by that time — out of here or dead, one of the two. Give me a hand!"

Their united efforts enabled them to drag the great negro into the master's room, and there they slumped him to the floor, a loose-mouthed, hideous mask of a man, more terrible than death in his enforced trance. Then they returned and brought in the judge. He had been struck sharply across the side of the head with a blackjack. The skin had been broken by the force of the blow, and a small trickle of crimson was running down his face. But otherwise he was uninjured, as Billy assured King Charlie.

"I tapped him careful — so careful it wouldn't have cracked the skull of a kid. But he sure has a paper head. He went down without so much as a gurgle. Here — he's coming to. Get a rope on his hands, will you?"

King Charlie, working with great deftness, threw a double loop over the wrists of the prisoner, and he opened his eyes to find himself helpless, with a revolver shoved under his chin.

"I'm dead — they've killed me — help, Johnson!" gasped Howick, as he sat up.

Then his senses clearing, he was suddenly aware of the gun and the masked man above him.

"Oh," he said, "I'm done for."

"You are," answered Billy English, "if you peep. Sit still, Howick. You're an old hand at cards, they say. Then you ought to know that this trick is ours, and it's against the rules for you to make a fuss when you haven't a chance. But I'll go a bit further and read out of the book to you. You mean, black-hearted rat, I've heard about the way you work. And you keep in mind that the only reason I don't cut your throat is because I hate to get my hands dirty. If you let out one yell, or if you try to bring attention of any kind here, I'll finish you, Howick, before I take another step. It'd be a pleasure — at that!"

Howick was silent, blinking into the face of the masked man and moistening his lips in a desperate effort to answer. Finally he forced the words out:

"I'll keep quiet, boys," he whispered. "You don't have to be afraid of me! I'll play the game now that I see I've lost!"

Billy English turned his back on the prisoner and kneeled beside the prostrate negro. He pushed up the eyelid of Jules and regarded the eye. Bowing his head he listened to the heartbeat and the breathing of the senseless man.

"Nothing could be better," murmured Billy. "He's doing fine. Won't wake up for an hour, maybe, and in the meantime he's having a fine sleep — no danger to him at all! But I thought it would be a thousand years before that big ox stopped wiggling, when I was holding the rag over his face. Where are the rest of the boys, Charlie?"

"They'll be here in a minute. They have to run around to this side of the house after they made the bluff to tackle them on that side. They'll come slow on the way into the patio. And —"

Here he stopped short, for a voice called from the patio, and then a footfall sounded in the hall: "We've drove 'em off, Mr. Howick, shall —"

Billy jammed his gun into the ribs of the rancher. "Stop that man!" he commanded.

"Who's there?" called Howick.

At once the footfalls stopped.

"Jordan."

"Go back to your place, Jordan. Who told you to come in?"

"Horn."

"Tell Horn to stay there."

"You don't want us to swing some men back to this side of the house?"

"No — I don't need advice. Get out!"

Hastily the footfalls retreated. The rancher looked up with despair toward his captors, and a moment later a huge, squat form filled the doorway, and Joe Hoyt was before them, with the lofty form of The Dean immediately behind him. The latter stalked at once toward Howick and then removed his mask.

"I been wearing this for the sake of some of the others, Howick," he said. "But when it comes to you, it sure goes to my heart to think of calling on you and going away without you having a chance to see my face. Here I am, Howick. I told you that I'd come back, and here I am to cheer you up and sit in at another little game with you."

Howick scowled fiercely up to him, but he returned no answer.

"Get up!" said The Dean and kicked Howick sharply. The latter started to his feet, his face convulsed with passion.

Here Billy English pressed close to The Dean and laid a hand on his arm.

"No more of that!" he commanded.

"The dog!" answered The Dean. "If I busted every bone in his body it would be less than what's coming to him!"

"Don't touch him," said Billy English ominously. "No matter what he is, he ain't to be touched while he's helpless. That's doing as bad as he done to you. Tell him what he's got to do, though."

"You're going down with us," said The Dean. "You're going to take us on a personally conducted tour into the cellar of La Casa Loma, son, and down there you're going to lead us into the room where you got the safe, and there you're going to work the combination for us and show us the way to the inside of your cash on hand. You understand?"

There was a faint, choked wail from the judge. But the protest died away when he had glanced at the savage face of The Dean.

"Fix that one, will you?" asked Billy of Joe Hoyt.

The big man stepped to the second captive. His ministrations were swift and effective. When he stepped back the private detective was bound hand and foot and gagged. He could neither rise from the chair nor cry out.

"Douse the light!" said Billy, putting out the one nearest to him, and in an instant the room was blanketed in the thickest darkness.

The victors filed off through the doorway with their captive.

CHAPTER XXX

JOHNSON'S DILEMMA

LEFT alone in the black room, poor Johnson meditated upon the fate which lay in store for him.

Five years before, for the commission of a petty act of theft, he had fallen under the shadow of the law and faced a prison sentence and a ruined reputation if his employer chose to prosecute the case. But here the rich rancher, Howick, had stepped in and saved him.

At first he had blessed the rancher, but he had been shown before long that Judge Howick never performed an act of charity. All that he did was done with a purpose, and the purpose now was to secure a private sleuth for his own uses. So Johnson had become the slave of the rancher.

His bonds were not heavy, and they rarely chafed, but always he was conscious that when the hour came he would be at the complete disposal of Howick. Even now he was liable to ruin, for if this adventure turned out as it now threatened to turn out, there was no question but that Howick would turn upon and tear all of those who were near him. He would first of all hate the man who had been the witness of his cringing and his humiliation. Yes, upon Johnson he would loose the full malignancy of his nature, and that, for the detective, meant destruction. So that he had not even the privilege of rejoicing whole-heartedly in the downfall of his master.

The only manner in which The Dean and his compeers could free him from dread would be by ending the existence of Howick, and he had heard too much from the lips of the master of the quartet, Billy English, to hope that the latter would allow a murder.

But if Howick could not be destroyed, he must be saved. There was no alternative, if Johnson hoped to save his own hide. So he turned over in his mind the possibilities. He was locked in a strong room, tied hand and foot and secured to a heavy chair. He was gagged so that his mouth and jaws ached, and he could barely breathe.

But in the room there was an agency which, if he could employ it, would at once set him free. That agency was big Jules. But Jules was tied in a manner no less effective than his. Yet he started hitching the chair across the floor. It was slow and heavy labor, and when he worked he began to breathe harder, and when he breathed harder the gag well-nigh choked him. Half throttled, his face swelling with the blood that rushed up toward his head, he nevertheless kept on, moving the chair an inch at a time, until his feet struck a soft mass. That must be Jules.

Yes, as he sat still and strove to regain his own breath, he could hear the breathing of the senseless negro. Then he raised his feet as well as he could, worked them down the leg of the negro and se- curing a bit of the flesh against the stone he ground down mercilessly.

It must have almost torn out the flesh like pinch- ers acting upon him. But still that agony did not rouse the negro. Johnson strove again. This time he succeeded in fetching a low groan from Jules. It was like the growl of a fierce dog, and now he desisted for a moment. What if the negro did return partially to his senses? Would he not at once attack the creature that tortured him? Mad- dened by the pain would he not fly at the throat of Johnson in the darkness?

For with no voice could Johnson reach the other. He could only wait and pray that the negro, if his brain cleared from the effects of the drug, would fumble about until he recognized the plight of the other man in the room and strive to liberate him, particularly since he might feel that it was the master who was in this condition.

An interval passed, and then Johnson ground his heel again into the flesh of Jules. There was a louder response this time, but still the body of the tortured man did not stir. Johnson sat back in his chair almost fainting with the suspense and the excitement. It was like prodding a wild tiger and hoping that he would spring the other way.

Finally, it might have been ten minutes or an hour, for all Johnson knew, the slumberer roused and sat up with a gasping oath. Johnson strove with all his might to speak. But he could not make a sound.

Then it seemed that the torment of the bruised places which Johnson's heels had made, fully brought back consciousness to Jules. He sprang to his feet. In the dark his sweeping hands struck the form of the bound man. He caught up Johnson, chair and all, and crashed him down to the floor, splintering the wood of the chair legs into a thousand shards.

That crashing noise seemed to bring back some of his senses to poor Jules. He fell upon his knees, moaning from the anguish of his tormented body. Then, fumbling with his great thick hands at the form of the silent man, he reached the cords, felt his way to the gagged mouth, and tore out the gag.

"Jules — thank God!" gasped the prisoner. "They've taken the master — they've taken Howick. He's down in the safe room in the cellar with the four of them. Get the rest of the boys! Quick!"

CHAPTER XXXI

HOWICK SHUTS THE DOOR

THE four and their prisoner had gone down the hallway to the patio, stolen along this under the shadows of the arcade to the stairway leading to the lower parts of the house, and then guided by the reluctant Howick, they went down into the musty darkness.

Here, lighting a lantern which he found hanging from the wall at one side, Howick seemed to regain some of his poise and his courage. As a matter of fact he was telling himself that if he could take the most indirect way of reaching the safe room, he would probably have taken so much time that some of his men might have a good chance of returning to his room, where they would find out what had happened.

It seemed impossible that he could be actually in the hands of four weak men, while a score of his own stanch fellows were within easy hailing distance. He could hardly believe the senses which told him that he was deliberately showing the way to the plunderers of his fortune. In the meantime he wound off to the side, taking the four through a long succession of store rooms and vacant chambers until finally the hand of

240

The Dean fell sharply upon his shoulders.

"Say, if you're killing time on us —" began the tall man.

That was all, but the rancher knew that he could gain no more in that manner. He conducted them, accordingly, straight to the door of the safe room. From the outside there was hardly a sign of a door, only an infinitesimal crack in the surface of the rock, for the door was simply a huge slab chiseled out of the side of the wall. The lock itself was set into the main body of stone and not into the door. Into it Howick fitted his key and presently the stone panel sagged in and a moist breath of cold air flowed slowly out around the four. Stepping inside they found themselves before a huge safe.

"Watch for the boards on each side of those two main doors that lead up to the front of the safe," cautioned the rancher. "They connect with levers that start water running into the cellar. In three minutes after the flow of water starts, the whole cellar is full to the top, and the gentlemen who call to see my safe are washed out. You understand?"

"Neat idea," said The Dean, "and, as a matter of fact, it sounds exactly like the sort of a plan you'd form, Howick. Now, the point is that the door is open, and that the water would run out of the cellar as fast as it would run in. But the next thing for you to do is to open the door. Don't try to tell us that you've forgot the combination!"

But the attitude of the rancher had undergone

a strange alteration. He no longer either cringed or snarled at them, but with perfect politeness he now said: "My friends, I have always fought hard, and I hate to lose, but when I see that I am hopelessly beaten, I trust that you will find me a good loser."

So saying, he fell upon his knees before the lock and worked at it busily for a moment. The tumblers clicked, and the heavy door swung slowly open. Inside they found themselves confronted with another and a smaller door.

"You see," said Howick politely, "that one blast would not have turned the trick with this safe of mine, and before a second blast could be set, I trust that the noise of the first one would have roused my men. But now that you have me with you, you don't need nitroglycerin."

Still smiling he worked at the combination on the smaller door, and when this also opened, he drew out a small steel drawer on either hand and extended them toward the four.

"Here you are," he said. "Here are the cash savings of my lifetime. Help yourself, boys. Then run through the rest of the safe, and you may find some other things of interest."

They gave him side glances, and then led by their greed, they snatched the drawers from him. As he had said, they were jammed with greenbacks. It was impossible even to estimate approximately so huge a sum of money, and, as they raised the lamp over it, the faces of the four showed curious differences in expression.

That of The Dean, for instance, showed the most fiery pleasure and gratification, as of one who deserves what he gets. King Charlie was frankly awed: Joe Hoyt was dazed; and only Billy English was for the moment saddened and seemed to be thinking of the possible consequences of this act.

It was he, too, who suddenly turned and cried: "Howick!"

On the instant his gun leaped into his hand. For Howick had slipped back toward the door, as the four leaned over the money. Now he checked himself on the very verge of leaping out and came back to them, giving the heavy door, as he did so, a passing twitch of sufficient strength to start it swinging shut.

"Get the door!" cried Billy English to Hoyt, who was nearest to it, but, as the slow-thinking giant did not instantly comprehend, he himself leaped like a flash for it. But he reached it just too late, for the heavy mass of rock shut, as his fingers reached for the edge. He seized the knob of the door and wrenched at it, but the lock closed with a spring. Then he whirled upon the rancher.

"Let's have your key!" he demanded.

And then he saw that Howick, white of face with excitement and malevolent pleasure, was standing with his arms akimbo and smiling upon them.

"Friends," said Howick, "I'm sorry to say that the key is on the far side of the wall. If you want it, dig through the wall with your finger nails and get it."

There was a stifled howl of rage and terror from Joe Hoyt, but, as he turned to throw himself at Howick, Billy English, always a master of the other three in the most rash moments of excitement, now interposed.

"Don't be a fool, Joe," he said. "Howick is only joking. He knows that we'd tear him to pieces if he didn't have some means of getting us out of here, and we'll put the screws to him until he tells us how."

"Fool?" asked Howick hoarsely, and he shook his triumphant fist in the face of the others. "I'll teach you how much of a fool I am! There's no other way to get out of this than to put a key into the lock, and I have no key. You can search me to the skin. Besides, there's no other way. Don't I know that if there were another way you'd tear it out of me? But no, my friends, the only way you leave this room is when the door is opened from the outside, and when that happens you can imagine who will be waiting for you on the opposite side of the wall. But if you try to even things up at my expense in the meantime — why, gentlemen, I need hardly tell you the difference between being sent to prison for robbery and being hanged for murder!"

All that he said was too entirely convincing. The money which they had stuffed into their pockets now became worse than useless. They flew at the door and wrenched at the knob, but the door merely quivered; and Joe Hoyt, recoiling, as his hand slipped off the knob, stepped back off the straight boards which led to the front of the safe. The boards upon which he staggered gave with a slight, metallic sound; there was a faint whirring of a powerful pump, and then a great stream of water began to crash upon the floor of the vault room.

There was a scream from Howick, all of whose assurance was stripped from him in a trice.

"You fool — you devil — we'll all drown like rats!"

CHAPTER XXXII

THE VAGABOND TRAIL

WHERE then was the courage of the stoutest of them? Howick was a raving, screaming coward, tearing at the wall with his bleeding finger tips. The tall Dean leaned against the safe with his face in his hands, and King Charlie stood gripping the hands of the dazed Billy English, as if the youngster who had saved them so often in crises could save them now.

Only Joe Hoyt showed the courage which makes men act. The water was rushing across the floor. In a trice it was up to their ankles. Then the lantern slipped from the hand of The Dean and was instantly extinguished.

A yell rose from the prisoners. With that tide of rapidly rising water, the rushing noise, and the choking darkness, it seemed that the bitterness of death was already theirs.

But big Joe Hoyt, too stupid and unimaginative to be crushed by his anticipations, waded forward through the deluge crying: "If we're going to get out, we got to get out by springing that lock, and if we spring that lock, I'm the man to do it. Lemme at it."

Fumbling forward he encountered the body of

246

Howick. He hurled the rancher aside with an oath, and the next instant his big hands were fixed upon the knob of the door. But the others, having heard his words, now gathered close behind him.

To none of them would it have occurred to attempt to break the spring of that lock by sheer pressure. Even with a jimmy they would have doubted their ability. But they had seen him do tremendous feats of strength before, and now they rallied close around him, while the water swirled at their hips and staggered them with the force of its current. Even the rancher scrambling back to them, was pinning his hopes on the strong man.

"The door's strong enough," he said; "but maybe the lock ain't so strong!"

"Try it!" called the others.

And Billy English, putting his hand upon the shoulders of the strong man, felt the shoulders turn to iron, as the muscles tightened with the effort. His whole great body quivered, there was a loud creaking noise, and then Joe Hoyt staggered back with a gasp. Water had risen to the height of the knob, and his grip had loosened and slipped off.

Water, indeed, was now swirling up to his shoulders, up to his chin. The scream of the rancher as he made out that Joe had failed, was a death cry.

But dauntless Joe Hoyt had still the courage of another effort. This time, stooping, the water covered the top of his head, while he fixed his mighty grip upon the knob of the door. Then, all immersed in the deluge, with his lungs heaving and burning under the suffocating strain, he heaved up again.

There was a wrench, a thin ray of light plunged through the darkness, and then the door was tugged in, and the water roared out into the hall beyond. They were free!

Another peril was on them, however, the moment the blessed light struck them; for the keen voice of the rancher was shrieking to his men, bidding them come to his aid, and trusting to the darkness to protect him from the wrath of the four.

It was the voice of Billy English which again saved him from destruction, as The Dean rose to shatter his skull and silence him with the blow of a revolver butt — the voice of Billy English commanding them all to rush on and hang together.

Staggering in the leaping current of the escaping water, they floundered to the first stairs and up these. As they did so, a door was wrenched open above them, and in the lighted square, they beheld the huge Jules, with Johnson beside him. They stood for an instant, amazed at the sight of the four hurrying up from below, all four dripping like half-drowned rats. Then they whipped up their guns.

But Billy English had drawn his weapon at the first showing of light, and while his three companions rushed blindly and frantically into the teeth of destruction, as if they hoped to smash their way to liberty by the sheer weight of numbers, he himself swerved to one side and, taking deliberate aim, now fired twice in quick succession.

The first bullet, nicely aimed, snapped the upper arm of Johnson. The second bullet, with hardly less accuracy, plowed through the thigh of the big negro. He went down with a crash, the gun exploding from his hand. He slid halfway to the bottom of the stairs, with a yell of pain and rage, and past him dashed the four and found the blessed air of the open night in the patio above them.

Half a minute too late Johnson had roused the negro from torpor.

But all of the circle around the house was now alive with the voices of shouting, cursing men who were beginning to realize that something was wrong, and who came rushing back as they heard the sudden crashing of firearms. Half a dozen of them swirled into the entrance to the patio, and Billy English pumped three shots in quick succession into the masonry beside them.

At the same time he shouted: "Hold the patio against them, boys. That's our chance!"

Now, as the men of the rancher tumbled back in alarm from the gateway, Billy turned to his companions.

"Start back through the rear of the house," he commanded.

"Back there? That's where they're all stationed now!" cried King Charlie.

"That's where they were a minute ago, you mean," answered Billy. "They'll be gone now. We'll slide through the gap. We can't make our own horses. Probably they got some of their own saddled. We got to pray for that. Dean and Hoyt, you run first, and I'll stay behind with King Charlie!"

With grunted acknowledgment that this was sound advice, the other two plunged away for the rear of the patio and then through a room, diving out of a window at the rear of La Casa Loma.

King Charlie and Billy English followed them as fast as the older limbs of the tramp would permit. But once outside the walls of the house they found themselves in a comparative silence.

There were shouts and guns exploding from the front, where it seemed that the men of the rancher were blocking the entrance to the patio and firing at random into its darkness. But they had not yet carefully spread the cordon around the whole building, and through the gap in the rear the fugitives ran in perfect safety until they reached the secondary shelter of the barns. There they found that there were no saddled horses, and at the same time two or three men from the house discovered them and started a heavy rifle fire.

King Charlie was detailed to hold the rear of the barn, confident that the rancher's men would never dare to rush across the open starlit space to get to close quarters with them. He kept up a steady fire, aiming at nothing, while the other three quickly selected three of the best horses, saddled them, and in another minute were under way.

As they went down the slope, they heard the screaming voice of Howick behind them offering ten thousand dollars a head for each of the four robbers. But they were off to a flying start, well mounted, in country adapted for a get-away. By the time the first gray of the dawn began to roll over the hills, they had dropped all signs of the pursuit far behind them.

"But where," asked Louise Alison Dora Young, "where does all this money come from that will send me to school?"

"Why," said Billy English, "I'll tell you about that. When your mother died, Lady, she left me quite a bunch of stuff — jewels and things. I turned all of that into money, and I soaked it away in mining stock. That sounds like a fool thing to do, eh? Well, the money was buried all these years, but just the other day it turned up that the mine had just struck pay dirt again, and now it's paying big."

"But then you'll go East with me, Uncle Billy?"

"How?"

"If there's as much money as that, we can surely go together!"

"Go on that money?"

He shook his head with a profound conviction. "The only thing that'll make that money good," he said, "is to spend it on you, honey. Besides, my place is out here riding herd!"

"Oh, well," she said, "my place is here, too, then. I'd be too lonely without you, Uncle Billy."

"That's fool talk — plumb fool talk!" he declared. "I've made up my mind about it — that's all, Lady. You're going East to school!"

Billy English was strangely silent for several days after Lady had been put on the train bound for the East. Even when King Charlie tried to get him interested in a new raid, he was singularly apathetic.

"No, King, I'm off the crook business for keeps," he declared with emphasis. "It's served its purpose. It's given me my stake to send Lady to school. Now I'm goin' to stick to cattle. It'll pay better in the long run."

The old tramp turned away with a sigh. It was a hard blow to him to lose this recruit whom he had started on the pathway of crime, but he saw keen, resolute determination in Billy's blue eyes and he knew from experience that argument was futile. He made a final despairing effort to make good his hold on this "son" whom he had won by deceit and fraud. He broke into a lengthy argument in which he drew an eloquent picture of his loneliness in the years ahead. But somehow his words did not carry conviction. The King's rôle of devoted father to Billy English had lost its powers of persuasion.

"You can stick around here as long as you want," said Billy in reply to one of his arguments. "No one's askin' you to leave. I ain't drivin' you away. But listen to this, King: It's no use tryin' to talk me into none of this long-ridin' business and bustin' into safes and holdin' up trains, 'cause from now on, I'm livin' fer Lady — an' I'm livin' straight. Get that!"

"But, son —"

"An' another thing, ol'-timer," Billy cut in, "go easy on that lovin' father sob stuff of yours. You've sung that old song altogether too much."

King Charlie heaved his broad shoulders and a deep sigh escaped him. He held out his hand.

"Then it's good-by, Billy," he said, and there was genuine emotion in his tone.

Billy English gripped the proffered hand. "If you *must* go, all right. And good luck to you!"

The King made a sweeping gesture. "You can't teach an old dog new tricks, Billy," he declared solemnly. "I've got to go on an' on an' on, till my last hour comes. I'm gettin' old, Billy, an' I was hopin' you'd stick by me till the end came. I can't stay put. I got to be movin'."

Billy English watched the stalwart old form swinging gallantly along the road with its tireless, mile-eating stride, that rolled so faultlessly from hip to heel and toe. King Charlie was traveling toward his kingdom of the steel rails and the rods and the blind baggage. There was only a slight pang of regret in the young man's heart. He was disillusioned with the life into which his associations with The King had led him. It had netted him enough of a stake to put Lady through school and to give himself a fair start with his cattle. But he realized that in the long run it did not pay. It had not paid in King Charlie's case; it would not pay in his case. He had Lady to live for — to make himself worthy in the years to come.

Now he could distinguish the tall form of King Charlie as he topped a distant rise. The gallant old vagabond was still swinging along with his smooth, easy stride, every step bringing him closer to the land of the rails and the rods where he found the zest and excitement and thrill of life. A moment later, he was out of sight.

"Well, King, if you really *are* my father," Billy English murmured to the vanished form of the old tramp, "you've given me somethin' to live down. But I'm goin' to live you down for Lady's sake!"

Max Brand is the best-known pen name of Frederick Faust, creator of Dr. Kildare, Destry, and many other fictional characters popular with readers and viewers worldwide. Faust wrote for a variety of audiences in many genres. His enormous output, totaling approximately thirty million words or the equivalent of 530 ordinary books, covered nearly every field: crime, fantasy, historical romance, espionage, Westerns, science fiction, adventure, animal stories, love, war, and fashionable society, big business and big medicine. Eighty motion pictures have been based on his work along with many radio and television programs. For good measure he also published four volumes of poetry. Perhaps no other author has reached more people in more different ways.

Born in Seattle in 1892, orphaned early, Faust grew up in the rural San Joaquin Valley of California. At Berkeley he became a student rebel and one-man literary movement, contributing prodigiously to all campus publications. Denied a degree because of unconventional conduct, he embarked on a series of adventures culminating in New York City where, after a period of near starvation, he recieved simultaneous recognition as a serious poet and successful popular-prose writer. Later, he traveled widely, making his home in New York, then in Florence, and finally in Los Angeles.

Once the United States entered the Second World War, Faust abandoned his lucrative writing career and his work as a screenwriter to serve as a war correspondent with the infantry in Italy, despite his fifty-one years and a bad heart. He was killed during a night attack on a hilltop village held by the German army. New books based on magazine seriels or unpublished manuscripts continue to appear. Alive and dead he has averaged a new one every four months for seventy-five years. In the U.S. alone nine publishers issue his work, plus many foreign countries. Yet, only recently have the full dimensions of this extraordinarily versatile and prolific writer come to be recognized and his stature as a protean literary figure in the 20th Century acknowledged. His popularity continues to grow throughout the world.